JUST A KISS

LYRICS AND LOVE
BOOK 4

SAMANTHA LIND

SAMANTHALIND.COM

Just A Kiss
Lyrics and Love Series Book 4
Copyright Samantha Lind 2022
All rights reserved.
Print ISBN: 978-1-956970-01-2

No part of this publication may be reproduced, transmitted, downloaded, distributed, stored in or introduced into any information storage or retrieval system, in any form or by any means, whether electronic, photocopying, mechanical or otherwise, without express permission of the publisher, except by a reviewer who may quote brief passages for review purposes. This book is a work of fiction. Names, characters, places, story lines and incidents are the product of the author's imagination or are used fictitiously. Any resemblances to actual persons, living or dead, events, locales or any events or occurrences are purely coincidental.

Trademarked names appear throughout this novel. These names are used in an editorial fashion, with no intentional infringement of the trademark owner's trademark(s).

The following story contains adult language and sexual situations and is intended for adult readers.

Cover Design by Oh So Novel
Cover image from Deposit Photos
Editing by *Amy Briggs ~ Briggs Consulting LLC*
Proofreading by *Proof Before You Publish*

❋ Created with Vellum

CONTENTS

Chapter 1	1
Chapter 2	12
Chapter 3	16
Chapter 4	24
Chapter 5	31
Chapter 6	39
Chapter 7	52
Chapter 8	57
Chapter 9	64
Chapter 10	69
Chapter 11	75
Chapter 12	83
Chapter 13	90
Chapter 14	100
Chapter 15	112
Chapter 16	120
Epilogue	126

Kiss Me or Not - Bonus Short Story	139
Chapter 2	141
Chapter 3	145
Chapter 4	155
Chapter 5	159
Chapter 6	165
Chapter 7	173
Chapter 8	177
Coming Soon	181
Also By Samantha Lind	183
Acknowledgments	185
About the Author	187

1

ALLISON

10 years ago
Junior year of high school

I sit at one of the many lunch tables filling the cafeteria, the one that my group of friends has claimed as ours over the last few years.

"Ugh," my best friend Lindsay says as she takes the seat next to me on the bench.

"What's wrong?" I ask as I take a bite from a chicken strip.

"History class sucked. We had a pop quiz, and I don't think I passed."

"I'm sorry, I hate it when Mr. Lead gives his pop quizzes. I swear he knows when we haven't done our homework and are not ready for them."

"Right! Like, help a girl out. Oh, I forgot to tell you!" Lindsay says, smacking my arm in quick succession in her excitement.

"What?" I ask, taking another bite.

"I have a date for prom!" she practically shrieks.

"With who? And when did this happen?" I ask, a little shocked.

"Jimmy King asked me to be his date after first period," she says.

"Aww," I coo. "You're going to have a blast."

"Now we just have to find you a date."

"Maybe. I was kind of looking forward to just going as a group, but maybe," I tell her honestly.

"I'm sorry. Should I back out so we can just go as a group?" she asks.

"No, it isn't like we won't see each other during the dance."

"Now I feel bad for saying yes so quickly."

"Don't be. I'll be fine," I insist.

"What about Lee? You guys have been quite flirty lately."

"Maybe," I state as a group of our friends sit down, Lee and Jimmy being two of them.

"Ladies," Jimmy greets as he takes the seat on the other side of Lindsay.

"I hear you've stolen my date for prom," I tease Jimmy.

"Sorry," he says, almost question-like and without one ounce of apology.

"You need a date to prom, Allison?" Lee asks from across the table.

"Looks like I do," I tell him, my stomach doing a little flittering when I look across the table at him. He's got this swagger to him. One that says he knows he's hot; he knows girls would fall at his feet if he'd give them a second of his time.

"Would you go with me?" he asks, all nonchalant.

"Are you serious?" I sputter in reply.

"Yes..." he says, drawing out the word. "Why wouldn't I be?"

"Sorry, I didn't mean it that way. I was just caught off guard," I tell him. "But I'd love to go with you." I flash him a sincere smile and melt a little at the way his face lights up.

"Oh-my-God!" Lindsay squeals and claps her hands together. "I'm so excited we're all pairing off for prom! We need to go dress shopping this week-end!" she says.

"Saturday work for you?" I ask.

"Yes, I have to work in the morning, but afterward, I'm all yours."

"I think my parents were arranging for a limo for the night, so if everyone wants to come to my place, we can all ride together," Lee says.

"Sounds like a plan," Jimmy replies.

"I'll be there," Tucker, another one of our friends, also replies.

"Who are you going with, Tucker?" I ask.

"Not sure yet, but I'm sure I can find a date," he says. He's got that same swagger that Lee has, and I've seen him turn on the charm. He'd have a date before the school day is over if he wanted one.

"That's my boy!" Lee says as they do that hand slap-hug-back slap thing guys do.

"I can't believe prom is just two weeks away already. It is going to be so lonely around here next year when you guys are all gone."

"No, it won't; y'all will be just fine being the rulers of the school," Tucker tells us.

I can't help being slightly jealous Lindsay and I aren't graduating this year, as well. We hope to go off to school together, maybe even rooming together if we're lucky enough. We both want to go to school and get our nursing degrees, then come back home and work either in the hospital or for one of the many doctors' offices.

The first bell rings, alerting us that it is time to clear out and head to our first class after lunch. We all say our goodbyes, parting ways until later. I practically float to my locker and then into my next classroom, knowing I'll be going to prom with Lee freaking Crawford.

Lee

I STRAIGHTEN MY COLLAR, ALLOWING ME TO BUTTON the top one up before wrapping the bow tie around my neck, securing it in place. Everyone should start arriving here shortly.

"Need any help?" my mom asks, standing at my open doorway.

"Sure," I say, handing over the cuff links my dad let me borrow for today.

Mom tugs my sleeves down, lining up the buttonholes before she slips the cuff links into them, securing them in place.

"I can't believe you're so grown up. Heading out to your senior prom, about to graduate and head out into the world." She sniffs, trying her damnedest to hold back her tears.

"Not going far, Mom, you know that," I remind her. Tucker and I plan to go to the fire academy in the fall.

"I know, but it's still weird knowing that you're about to move out on your own. I'll miss you at the dinner table every night."

"If it's dinner that you're worried about, I can make sure to be home every night for that," I tease. Nothing in this world like my mom's cooking.

"I definitely wouldn't put it past you to do just that." She laughs.

"You know me, I'll do just about anything for a free meal." I wink at her.

"I love you, son." She pulls me into a hug, and I go willingly. I tower over her, but she doesn't care. I hold her tight against my chest. I've always had a great relationship with my parents. They've always been pretty chill. They set the rules, and as long as we follow them, they give us a lot of freedom.

"Love you, too, Mom." I kiss the top of her head, choking back my own tears.

"Oh, a Momma Crawford sandwich," Tucker says, coming into my room and wrapping his arms around my mother, trapping her between us.

"You boys." She laughs. "My life would be so empty without you."

Tucker steps back, allowing Mom to vacate her spot. She looks both of us up and down, tears rolling down her cheeks as she does. "I just can't get over how grown the two of you are," she says, patting us both on the chest.

"Believe it, Momma Crawford. Before you know it, we'll be grown men with families of our own," Tucker says.

"Speak for yourself, dude. I don't plan on settling down anytime soon."

"I'm not saying tomorrow, but in the next five to ten years, I'll bet you money that at least one of us has a wife and or kids."

"I'll leave that domestic shit to you."

"Language!" Mom chides.

"Sorry, ma'am."

"I'm going to leave you boys to finish getting ready. Just remember tonight is all about having fun, but not *too* much fun. We don't need any babies coming as a result of the fun tonight."

We both watch Mom leave the room, a little slack-jawed at her comment.

"Did she just say what I think she said?" Tucker asks, pointing to the doorway she just exited from.

"Yep, so at this point, I won't be shocked if she hands us condoms before we leave for the night."

"Dude." He smacks my chest. "I can't go there. I just can't think of sex and your mom in the same thought. If she hands us condoms, all I'll be able to think of when ripping it open is her saying not to make a baby tonight."

"Same," I agree.

Thankfully, we're pulled from this awkward as fuck conversation by voices downstairs. We both grab our suit jackets and head downstairs, joining the rest of our friends who have shown up. I about swallow my tongue when I see Allison in her hot as hell dress. The slit up her left thigh has my dick twitching in my slacks. The way the top shows off the pillowy tops of her breasts has me wanting to lay my head on them and never leave. What I wouldn't do to just tug that fabric down and suck on her nipples. I wonder if I could get her off just from nipple stimulation? I shake my head, needing to clear my thoughts from sex and a naked Allison before I'm pitching a tent in my pants and everyone knows where my thoughts are at right now.

"Hi," she shyly greets, coming to stand right in front of me.

"You're beautiful," I tell her, reaching out and

running a finger down her cheek, onto her neck, then across her collar bone. I stop myself from running it down over her breasts – one, because we have an audience, and two, because she isn't mine. We aren't dating, have never kissed, or even talked about anything like that. I just took a shot by asking her last week and was shocked when she agreed so quickly.

"Thanks," she says, blushing as her eyes drop down my body. "You clean up pretty well yourself."

"I try."

"Let's get all of you lined up for some pictures before the limo arrives," Mom calls out.

We all follow her outside, lining up as she instructs, taking hundreds of pictures for everyone's parents. Our yard is a hopping place for the next half hour, but we all have a good time joking as we do as told.

Once we're all in the limo, I clear my throat, getting everyone's attention on our way to dinner. "I'd like to make a toast, of sorts," I say, holding up one of the small water bottles the limo company places in the back for guests. "To a night of fun, let's end this year on a high note. Stay safe, everyone."

"Hell yes!" a few of the guys call out.

As the opening chords of *Just the Way You Are* by Bruno Mars starts over the PA system, I tug Allison out onto the dance floor. I've been itching to get my hands on her body all night. We've held hands, and she was pressed to my side in the limo, but I want to keep her in my arms. Feel her body pressed against mine.

"Having fun?" I ask once we've found a spot to start swaying together. She's wrapped her arms up and around my neck while mine are firmly on the small of her back. There's only an ounce or so of space between our bodies, something I hope to close as the night goes on.

"Of course, and you?" she asks.

"The best," I tell her honestly. "Only one thing that would make it better," I find myself saying.

"What's that?" she asks before biting her bottom lip slightly.

"If I was kissing you right now."

"What's stopping you?"

"Nothing, now." I lean down, tentatively swiping my lips across hers. She tugs me closer, and I take advantage. I bring my hands up to cup her cheeks, angling her head ever so slightly, which allows me to deepen the kiss. She opens to me instantly, and the sparks I feel are life-changing. Why did I wait so long to take this girl out? I've only crushed on her for the last two years.

"Wow," Allison says when we break apart. She presses her fingers over her kiss-swollen lips, and I can't help but be proud of the fact that I'm the reason they're so swollen. "That was..." She trails off.

"The best first kiss ever," I finish for her.

"Yes," she agrees.

2

ALLISON

Present day

I PLOP DOWN ON MY COUCH, A GLASS OF WINE IN ONE hand and a warm, gooey brownie in the other.

"Ugh, today sucked," Lindsay says, joining me on the couch with her own brownie and glass of wine.

"You can say that again. I don't think I ever had a break. I'm shocked that I even had time to pee."

"Same, girl. I think I'm going to sleep straight through these next three days off."

"I wish. I've got shit to get done that I keep putting off," I tell her. "I also kinda want to go out dancing tomorrow night. Blow off some steam; what do you say we go hit up ladies' night?"

"I could probably be talked into it," Lindsay says.

"It's a date, then."

"Is this a-dance until you find a cute guy that will take you home and rock your world kind of night-, or just a go have fun and come home alone to your vibrator kind of night?" Lindsay asks.

"I haven't decided. I wouldn't turn away some good dick right about now. Maybe that is what I need in this lonely life of mine."

"You and me both, sister."

"The single life is for the birds. We need to do something about this sad state of our lives," I say.

"Why do all the good ones have to be taken already? I don't need just another fuck boy," Lindsay adds.

"Amen to that. What's the likelihood we both find that before kissing another hundred frogs?"

"Put that shit out in the universe, and we'll manifest it."

"Universe, if you're listening, I want a man who isn't into playing games, has a slightly larger than average dick, and knows how to use it, along with his tongue, if I'm allowed to be specific. One that wants a long-term commitment, a family down the road, hell, even the white picket fence, and a dog or two. One that has a full-time job and preferably doesn't live in his parents' basement. Oh, and six foot-plus and fit. Thank you, universe," I project my wishes.

"Nice," Lindsay says.

"Now, it's your turn. Let's manifest this shit."

"Universe, I'd like a family man, one who's more interested in coming home every night than hitting the bar. Someone who knows how to treat a woman, yet is freaky in the bedroom. I'm not too picky on height, just as long as he's my height or taller. Someone that can hold me tight in his arms, protect me when needed, be my strength when I need it, yet allow me to be his when he is the one in need."

"Damn, girl, I hope for the both of us that this works. We both deserve it so much." I pull my bestie into a side hug. We both stay leaning against one another as we finish off our glasses of wine.

"I guess I should head home," Lindsay says, stretching before she stands up. "I'm turning off my alarms, silencing my phone, and sleeping in as late as my body will let me."

"That sounds like the best plan." I follow her to the door. She slips her sandals on, then gives me a hug before heading out the door. "I'll text you once I'm up, and we can make plans for Joe's tomorrow night."

"Sounds good!" she calls back before disappearing down the hall.

I close the door, flipping the deadbolt before heading back into my living room. I collect our dirty glasses and trash, taking everything into the kitchen. I clean up the few things that are out, starting the dishwasher so that I don't have to do it tomorrow. I pour the last glass of wine from the bottle into my glass, then toss the bottle into the recycling bin.

With the kitchen clean, I take my wine with me and head for my bedroom. A nice relaxing bath after a long-ass shift in the ER is calling my name. I turn on the water, letting the tub fill with hot-steamy water. Once it is high enough, I kick on the jets and toss in some soothing bath salts before stripping from my scrubs. I snag my kindle from my nightstand, placing it on the little tray that fits across my tub that Lindsay got me for Christmas last year. It has a tiny slot to hold up a book or, in my case, my kindle, and a place for my drink. No spilling is happening tonight. I also reach into one of the vanity drawers, grabbing one of my little waterproof vibrators. With the spice level of my current read, it wouldn't surprise me if I needed to take care of business while in the tub.

3

LEE

I walk into Joe's, and it is already a busy place tonight. Ladies' night is usually this way. People are ready for the end of the week, ready to kick off the weekend a day early. I push my way to the bar, flagging down Joe when he looks my way.

"What can I get you tonight?" he asks, setting a napkin down on the bar in front of me.

"I'll take a Blue Moon on tap," I tell him, handing over a ten-dollar bill. He quickly fills the chilled glass, adding an orange slice to the top. He sets it down, along with my change. I grab the drink, leaving a couple bucks' tip on the counter for him. Joe's always been a good guy.

I turn around looking for anyone I know. Tucker

wasn't sure if he'd make it tonight, daddy duty and all that. I don't begrudge the guy. His daughter Paisley is his world, as she should be. She's a firecracker and keeps him on his toes, but he wouldn't change it for anything. She might have been a surprise, but she's been the best thing to happen to him.

I see a few of the other guys from the station all holding down a table along the edge of the dance floor, so I make my way through the crowd and join them.

"You made it," Jack, one of the guys on a different shift than I am, says. I shake his hand, slapping him on the back in a bro hug.

"How've you been, man?" I ask genuinely.

"Eh, hanging in there. Life's been stressful, but I'll make it through."

"Sorry to hear that. How's Rachel?"

He rubs a hand along his neck before blowing out a breath. "She filed for divorce about three months ago," he tells me.

"Fuck, sorry about that, man."

"Yeah, it was a shock to me, as well," he says before downing the rest of his beer. "I guess I missed all the signs."

"Things getting nasty?" I ask. I've heard of way

too many horror stories from other guys from the station who've gone through divorces.

"Thankfully, we're staying pretty friendly. Not having any kids makes things a thousand times easier. At this point, it is just a matter of waiting on the courts to process all the paperwork. We easily split our assets and went our own ways. I just never thought I'd be thirty and divorced."

"Welcome back to the single life, man. It isn't all that bad," I tell him.

"If you say so. There's something about having someone you can count on at home every night."

"But is the heartbreak worth it when they decide it isn't worth the fight?" I question.

He accepts another beer from the waitress, taking a healthy drink from it before answering me. "I guess that depends. Not every relationship ends as mine did. So, I'd like to think that I'd have still gone after Rachel all those years ago, even knowing the outcome. We had a lot of good times together. We just weren't meant for forever."

"You're braver than me," I tell him. "I don't think I'll ever settle down."

"Never say never," he says.

I look over to the dance floor, a few friends from high school catching my eye. One specific person—Allison. Now that's a woman that could pull me in and wrap me up in her. My mind wanders back all those years to my senior prom, when she was my date. I still think back to that kiss we shared on the dance floor. We didn't take things any further that night, but I've dreamed for ten years what it would be like to get a second chance at another kiss or, even better, a night in my bed.

"Need a napkin for all that drool?" Jack asks.

"Fuck off." I laugh. "I wasn't drooling."

"Could have fooled me." He smirks. "Why don't you go over there and ask her to dance?"

"No, she's off-limits. Definitely one of the good ones that are looking for a forever kind of man."

"The good ones are worth it, man. If I can still believe that, then so can you."

I don't reply; I just take a drink of my beer. I watch as Allison and Lindsay shake their asses to the music, laughing as they have a great time out on the dance floor.

The song ends and they head for the bar. I follow behind them, pushing my way to the bar next to them. Joe comes over, taking their order before nodding to my empty glass. I hand him my card. "I'll get these ladies' drinks this round," I tell him.

"Lee." Lindsay turns to me. "You didn't have to do that but thank you."

"Anytime. Are you ladies having a good time tonight?" I ask.

"Yes!" Allison calls out. "It was one hell of a week, and this is just what we needed tonight."

"Busy days in the ER?" I ask. I could smack myself upside the head at that stupid question.

"I swear it was a full moon all week. We had the busiest shifts we've had in a long-ass time."

"I understand completely. We went out on more calls this past week than we usually do."

"It was something. I'm just thankful for a few days off."

"Me too," I agree with them. "Do you ladies have a table? You're welcome to join us over at ours," I offer up.

"Thanks, we'll do that," Lindsay says. Joe returns with our three drinks and my card. I quickly sign the slip before tucking my card into my wallet and leading the ladies back to our table.

I make quick introductions when we reach the table. Due to our jobs—the ladies being ER nurses, and all of us guys being EMTs or firefighters—our paths often cross when we're dropping patients off at the hospital.

Lindsay falls into a conversation with a few of the guys about someone they brought in the other day, which gives me the perfect opportunity to talk to Allison.

"How've you been?" I ask.

"Oh, you know, the usual. Work, sleep, laundry, repeat. How about you?"

"Pretty much the same."

"How are your parents doing these days?" she asks.

I can't help but smile at the mention of my parents. "They're doing good; Mom retired at the end of last school year. I don't think it has quite hit her yet that when the summer ends, she'll not be returning to the school."

"Good for her! Is your dad retiring anytime soon?"

"Not for another few years. Mom's going to be helping my sister and her husband out with babysitting their new baby."

"Aww, when did Alley have a baby?" she asks, and I can tell she genuinely wants to know.

"About a month ago, a little girl," I tell her, pulling my cell out to pull up one of the pictures of my sister and niece.

"Oh, she's so precious! Tell her I said congratulations!"

"I'll do that."

"So, what else is new with you? Still proclaiming the bachelor life?" she asks.

"You know it." I wink at her.

"Some woman is going to rock your world one of these days, and you're going to fall head over heels in love with her, and I can't wait to watch. It's always the ones that protest the most that fall the hardest."

"Nah," I proclaim. I take another swig from my beer before expanding my reply. "Only if that woman is you," I tell her.

"Me?" she questions. "Why me?"

"Please don't break my heart and tell me I'm the only one that felt those sparks between us all those years ago at prom? I still compare every kiss to that one," I tell her honestly.

"Oh," she says, and I can tell that I've shocked her. "I've always figured I was the only one to remember that moment."

"Sweetheart, please. That was one of the best nights of my life," I tell her, stepping into her space. "And given a chance, I'd do it--and hopefully a lot more--all over again. Preferably multiple times." I smirk, hopefully getting my point across.

I don't miss the way her cheeks flush red as her blush creeps up her neck. Seeing her skin change color has my mind running with thoughts of what it looks like when she's about to come. My cock swells in my jeans, pressing hard against my zipper as it looks to bust out.

"Hmmm, I'll have to remember that," she finally says, and I can practically hear her thinking.

Our conversation is interrupted when Lindsay asks Allison a question. I could almost throttle her for butting in at this moment, but I just go with the flow. The ladies end up back out on the dance floor, and I'm left here to nurse my beer and my deflating cock for the rest of the night.

4

———————

ALLISON

Two months later

I CAN'T BELIEVE SUMMER IS OVER AND FALL IS starting to make its appearance. Don't get me wrong; I'll gladly take the slightly cooler days. Give me a chunky sweater and boots weather, and I'm all over it.

"Are you ready yet?" I call out to Lindsay as she applies her mascara. I enter her bathroom and sit on the closed toilet while waiting for her to finish up.

"Yep," she says as she cleans up her makeup.

"It's just Joe's; you don't have to look perfect," I remind her, referring to the local bar we're headed out to tonight. We're meeting a few other friends there for a drink or two. It's ladies' night, and it has been one hell of a week at work again.

"All right, let's go," Lindsay says before grabbing her debit card and driver's license from her wallet and sliding them into a tiny little wristlet, along with some cash and some Chapstick.

"I can't wait to get out on the dance floor and shake our asses off tonight," I say on the way to the bar; the drive isn't far from Lindsay's little house.

"I know. I need to release some steam, and a drink or two, and some time on the dance floor sounds like the perfect way to unwind," Lindsay agrees with me.

"And not having to work tomorrow is the perfect excuse to let loose tonight," I add as Lindsay pulls into the parking lot. Ladies' night is sometimes more popular of a night than Friday and Saturday nights can be, and by the looks of how full the parking lot is already, tonight is going to be that way. "The one thing better that I can think of to let off some steam would be some good dick, but I don't think that's on either of our horizons tonight."

"God, what I wouldn't do with some good dick," Lindsay agrees.

"I mean, I'm sure you could easily find a man or two that'd gladly take you home for a fun night between the sheets," I tell her, bouncing my eyebrows up and down as she laughs.

"Not that desperate," she says. "Yet," she adds for good measure.

"Girl, you need to live a little. A good one-night stand might do you good. There's just something about some no-strings-attached sex that will set you up for a few weeks."

"Yeah, I'm still just fine for now. I've got a few other BOBs to keep me company on lonely nights," she says.

"Girl, tell me about it. Sometimes you've got to do what you've got to do."

We make it inside the bar, looking around for the group of friends we're supposed to meet here tonight. I see a few of them already at a table. Since we live in a small town, it isn't like I don't know just about everyone here, and just like high school, everyone is grouped off. Lindsay and I stop off at the bar; Joe's working tonight.

"What can I get you ladies tonight?" he asks, wiping the bar top in front of us off before placing down two cocktail napkins.

"I'll take whatever light beer you've got on tap," I tell him.

"I'll have a raspberry mojito, please," Lindsay states.

"Coming right up," he says, reaching for a glass to put under the beer tap to fill my beer up first. "You ladies want a tab tonight?" he asks, setting my glass down in front of me.

"Yep," I say. "And we'll be over there." I point at the table that already has six or so people around it. From this angle, it's hard to tell if they're all at one table or if some of them are part of the next table and just chatting with our group.

We reach the table and find our friends, Becky, her husband Todd, Rob, David, and his girlfriend, Trisha. At the table next to them are some other guys, Tucker and Lee, along with a couple of other guys I recognize as firefighters that work with Tucker and Lee. Working in the ER, we see the paramedics and firefighters regularly.

"You made it!" Becky calls out, hopping off the barstool she was perched on to give Lindsay and me hugs.

"Of course!" Lindsay calls out over the music already playing. "Wouldn't miss ladies' night for anything." I say my hellos around the group before making my way over to Lee and Tucker's table. Lee and

I have been flirting for months, it feels. I don't think that I would turn him down if he asked me back to his place tonight. The anticipation of something more with him has been buzzing in my blood, and I just don't think I have it in me to tell him no any longer.

"Hey," I greet the guys. I set my beer down on their table and try to act as naturally as possible.

"Evening," Tucker greets, his deep voice would make most women's panties wet, but it just doesn't do it for me.

"Lee," I say, his name coming out almost like a moan.

"Evening, Allison," he greets, before taking a pull from his beer. "How's it going tonight?" he asks once he's swallowed the beer. I admit, I watched the way his Adam's apple bobbed as he did so. It's amazing what can look sexy on a man when all you want to do is strip him naked and suck his cock, before riding it until you're both so far gone, you can't see anything but the stars behind your eyelids.

He clears his throat, and I realize I didn't catch anything he said. The smirk on his lips tells me that he knows exactly where my mind just was. On that note, I turn to the table with all my girls and call out, "Are you ready to shake your asses?" The opening chords of "Champagne Night" by Lady A come on, and we all head for the dance floor and start dancing.

As we dance the night away, I constantly feel like I've got a set of eyes on me. I look around, spotting Lee still at the table with Tucker. His eyes are solely on me tonight, which makes me want to drive him crazy. I roll my body against Lindsay's to the beat of the music, and can tell—even from across the bar— that my movements affect him. I watch as he, not so discretely, reaches down and adjusts himself. What I wouldn't do to be that beer bottle in his hands. The one that he keeps bringing to his lips with each pull he takes from it.

We dance for what feels like forever before the DJ changes things up and slows them down. I head for the bar, needing some water before I order another beer. While I'm waiting for Joe, I turn and lean against the bar top, which allows me to look out over the dance floor. I notice that Tucker has finally manned up and is out dancing with Lindsay. I've been pretty sure that he's been holding back an attraction to her since we were in high school, but nothing ever came of it. I think they'd be perfect for each other.

"Didn't want to stick it out on the dance floor?" Lee asks from where he's found space next to me. I was so engrossed in watching my best friend out on the dance floor that I missed him approaching the bar.

"Uh, no," I tell him. "I'm not into the slow shit."

"Is that so?" He smirks, and I walked myself right into that innuendo.

"That's right, I like it fast-paced, rough, and to keep me going all night long," I boldly tell him as I turn to face him. He steps into my personal space, our faces only an inch or so apart. Our breaths mingle as we both stand here facing one another, waiting on the other to make a move.

He brings his hand up, trailing a fingertip from my cheek, down my neck, and into my exposed cleavage. "Come home with me," he states more than asks.

I can practically hear my resolve snap. I don't know if it is the alcohol—although I haven't had much yet tonight—or the building sexual tension that has been developing between Lee and me, especially the last few months, but I take a leap of faith— or stupidity. I guess tomorrow morning will decide. "Okay," I agree.

"Really?" he questions. I guess he really was used to me always turning him down; it almost makes tonight all that more special.

5

LEE

I'M STILL A LITTLE FLABBERGASTED THAT ALLISON SAID yes when I asked her to come home with me. She's always turned me down in the past. I've almost felt like this back and forth flirting with each other has become a game between us. One that never ends with either of us getting anywhere further than a little more sexually frustrated.

"Really?" I question. I need to make sure she's making a clear decision.

"Stop overthinking it and take me home, Lee," she commands, and I like it when she's a little feisty.

We walk back over to the table, and I toss a couple of twenties down to help cover my beer and the tip.

"I'm ready to call it a night; how about you?"

Lindsay asks Allison. All the girls met us back at the table as we approached.

"I think I'm going to go home with Lee. Are you good to get yourself home?" Allison asks, chewing on her bottom lip as she hangs onto my side. My arm is firmly around her waist, a bit possessively. I want every guy in this place to know that she's going home with me.

"I'm good, be safe, and call me if you need anything," Lindsay tells Allison.

"I'm good," she assures Lindsay. "Text me to let me know when you make it home."

"Yes, Mom." Allison rolls her eyes at Lindsay, laughing as she does. I love seeing the easy camaraderie between these two women. They were as thick as thieves back in high school, and it doesn't look like they've lost that at all.

"Don't give me no sass, young lady," Allison retorts back. "Are you good to drive?" she asks, all joking aside.

"I can give you a ride if you need one," Tucker slides into the conversation. "I only had one beer, and that was hours ago," he tells them, and I know he's not lying.

"I'm good. I only had two drinks all night and a few glasses of water. I can get myself home, but thanks for the offer," Lindsay tells him as she turns in his direction and smiles up at him. I know my best friend well enough to know that he's digging her and wants so bad to make a move; he just hasn't made it happen yet.

"Okay," he concedes.

"Be safe, y'all. And don't do anything stupid," Lindsay says, turning her sights on Allison and me.

"Yeah, wrap that shit up," Tucker says before slapping me on the back. I take that as our cue to exit stage left and get the hell out of this bar.

***

It doesn't take long before we're in my truck and on our way to my place.

I reach over in the dark cab of my truck and find Allison's warm thigh. My hand fits perfectly over it, almost as if it was made for me. She rests her hand over mine, drawing small circles on the back of my hand with her fingertips.

The ride to my place is silent, except for the old country music coming from the speakers. The way Tim McGraw croons on about not taking the girl from him. Brings back memories from my childhood and listening to this song.

I pull into my driveway, parking the truck outside of my garage. I have it filled with some wood I'm using to make my mom some things she's asked for. I kill the engine, then give Allison's thigh a squeeze before I open my door and hop out. I've almost made it around to the passenger side when she pops the door open and slides out.

I tuck a strand of her hair behind her ear as we stand outside, staring at one another. The moon and stars are out tonight, as is a brisk chill in the air. I shiver as the cold pushes past my thin layers of clothing. "Let's get inside where it isn't so damn cold," I suggest. I slide my hand into hers, and sparks shoot straight up my arm from our contact.

She walks beside me as we make our way inside my house. I flip on the lights as soon as we enter the front door. Once Allison is inside, I close the door behind us, flipping the deadbolt out of habit.

"Would you like something to drink?" I ask, my manners not getting far from me.

"Sure, what do you have?" she asks, and I detect a hint of nerves.

"Water, beer, maybe some juice, and a pop or two," I tell her as I make my way into the kitchen and open the fridge.

"Pop or water is fine," she says, following me.

I grab her a Dr Pepper, popping the top before I hand it over. I reach back into the fridge and grab a bottle of water for myself.

I lean against the counter, facing Allison as she stands just inside the doorway of the kitchen. I drink her in, from the tips of her toes to the top of her head. She's always been sexy to me. The quintessential girl next door with the natural beauty. She looks just as good with her hair up in a messy bun and no makeup as she does when she's all dressed up and ready to hit the town. I swear she never had an awkward adolescent stage like most of us had.

Allison steps to the side, leaning against the doorframe, and mirrors my stance. We're now in a staring contest. The air between us practically crackles with the sexual tension. We've been dancing around this for months, years if you want to go all the way back to high school, when my attraction for this woman really started.

"Why are you standing all the way over there?" she finally asks, taking a sip of her pop.

"I thought you might back out for a moment there. I was just trying to give you some space if you needed it," I tell her as I set my water down on the counter. I quickly close the few feet of distance between the two of us. I stop only once I'm inches from her, the palms of my hands resting against the wall behind her as I box her in.

I tower over her by a few inches, and with us this close, she has to crane her neck to look up at me. I smirk as I tilt my head down, bringing our lips close enough they're almost touching.

"Tell me what you want tonight," I request. "I need to know your boundaries," I add before she can reply.

"My-my boundaries?" she questions, but I don't miss the flash of heat in her eyes. Her mind went straight to the gutter, and I'm here for that kind of thing. "Do you mean, like, kinky shit?" She scrunches her nose up.

I can't help but laugh at her question. "Maybe, but mostly what you're hoping will happen tonight. What is on the table, and what's a no-go. I don't want either of us to be on different pages," I tell her honestly. I always make sure women know the score before anything happens. I'm a one-night kind of guy. I'll rock their world as much as they can manage, that one night, but that's where it ends. I'm not a seconds kind of guy, usually.

"I'm here for you to fuck me, Lee. I thought that was pretty clear when I agreed to come home with you."

I puff out a breath in a half bark of laughter at her crass words. If there is anything that Allison does well, it is not beat around the bush. She's as straightforward as they come.

"Do you like blindfolds? Silk ties?" I ask, as I'm curious how spicy or vanilla she likes things.

"I've never tried them," she says, and I don't miss the hint of redness in her cheeks as they blush. "But I'd be interested in trying them sometime. With the right partner, that is. One I know that I can trust with my life," she quickly adds.

"Kink play definitely comes with a high level of trust. From both partners involved."

"I can only imagine," she muses. "So, does that mean that you like those types of things?" she asks.

"Yes, but I don't use them often. As I said, they require a high level of trust, and you don't get that with one-night stands very often."

"Maybe we can change that," she says before pushing up on her toes slightly and bringing our lips together.

I deepen the kiss, pinning her against the wall, our bodies flush together. Her hands are all over my chest, back, arms. I hike one of her legs over my hip, allowing me to grind against her center in the most delicious way. Finding a little friction for my hardening cock. I can feel her heat, even with all the fabric between us.

I bring a hand up to her breasts, tweaking a nipple through the fabric and pulling a moan from her. I swallow the sound, not letting up on my exploration of her body. The way it perfectly fits with my own is mind-boggling, but something I don't stop to think much about. The feeling of this woman in my arms, kissing me back while I practically maul her, is a heady feeling.

"Take me to your bed," she requests when we break for a short breath. I don't need to be asked twice, so I scoop her up in my arms and carry her down the hall and into the master. I deposit her on the edge of the bed, dropping a chaste kiss to her lips before I stand to my full height. I lean over and flick the bedside lamp on, giving us a nice glow of light that isn't harsh like the overhead ones.

I quickly pull my T-shirt off over my head, tossing it into the basket along the wall. I unbuckle my belt and undo the top button of my jeans. I watch as Allison tracks each of my moves. The desire I can see in her eyes spurs me on to keep going. She wants this. I want this. It's only been ten or so years in the making. I just hope this doesn't fuck up our friendship.

6

———

ALLISON

I sit on the edge of Lee's bed. The anticipation of what he'll do next is killing me. I just want him to be touching me. To have his lips on mine or somewhere else on my body is the ultimate goal for tonight. Well, that and to have one of his specific appendages inside me at some point, maybe multiple times before the night is over, if we're lucky.

I don't know what is sexier, the bare chest or the unbuckled and unbuttoned jeans with a belt still attached. With the top open, I can see the top inch or so of his black boxer briefs. The tip of his swollen cock is inching closer to the elastic band. I lick my lips, thinking of what it would be like to take him into my mouth.

"You're going to kill me if you keep looking at my

dick like that," Lee announces. My own arousal pools in my panties, and I can't help but rub my thighs together, looking for some kind of friction to provide me some pleasure.

"Then come closer, and I'll stop looking and start touching," I boldly tell him.

"You are a little vixen, aren't you?" he asks, stepping between my open thighs. I lay back on my elbows, and he follows until he's hovering over me. I take advantage of him standing between my thighs and wrap my legs around his hips, bringing him even closer to my center.

"I can be; I just need the right man to bring it out of me," I tell him before pulling his head down so our lips meet.

He kisses me deeply. So deep I practically feel it down to my soul. He kisses me in a way that no man, other than when he was seventeen years old, has kissed me.

It doesn't take long before he's trailing kisses down my neck, sucking lightly to the sensitive areas as he maps everything with his mouth. When he reaches the collar of my shirt, he pulls back and looks down at me, a crooked grin on his lips. "You're a little overdressed, don't you think?"

I reach down and find the hem of my top. I

quickly pull it up and over my head, leaving me in my bra on top and jeans and panties on bottom. He easily undoes the top button on my jeans, then slowly lowers the zipper. It all happens in slow motion, but also fast. It's like I'm watching from the outside looking in. My senses are on high alert so that my body doesn't really know what to focus on.

"You still with me?" he asks.

"Of course," I tell him as I lift my hips off the bed so he can slip my jeans over them. I don't miss the fact that he leaves my panties in place. He drops his jeans, as well, but keeps the boxer briefs.

"Fuck, you're even more gorgeous than I ever imagined," he tells me, his voice all deep and gravely now.

He leans back down, taking my nipple into his mouth, the fabric of my bra still between us. The lace rubbing against my skin as his tongue laps at me applies an extra layer of stimulation. He deftly slides a hand behind my back, flicking the clasp open. He grabs the fabric with his teeth, pulling it away from my body until he can fling it entirely out of the way.

With my breasts completely exposed to him, he cups them both before leaning back down and licking at each nipple. He alternates, keeping a steady pace as they harden under his touch.

I close my eyes and let the sensation wash over me. The amount of pleasure I'm feeling, and he's only at my breasts. It's almost embarrassing how close to coming I am already.

"You like that?" he says against my skin, and I can't help but arch into his touch.

"Yes," I pant. I run my fingers through his hair, holding his head tight against my body. He slides down, nipping at the underside of my breasts before looking up at me.

"I can't wait to fuck these later tonight," he says, holding my breasts together and creating the perfect space for his cock to slide in. I've never done that with a guy, but there's always a first time for everything.

"We'll see." That is all I can think to say, and I don't miss the smirk that crosses his lips before they go back to mapping my exposed skin.

He takes his sweet-ass time, making his way to the waistband of my panties. They sit low, seeing as how they're bikini cut, so he's practically an inch or so above my clit.

"Can I kiss you here?" he asks, rubbing a finger lightly over my mound and down my slit.

"I'd kick you out of your own bedroom if you didn't," I tell him. He's teased me for what feels like forever. I'm practically ready to crawl out of my own body; I'm strung so tightly at this point. I need some more action and a release like I need my next breath.

"If you kicked me out, I couldn't give you multiple orgasms tonight," he muses.

"Touché." I shrug. "So, what are you waiting on, then? An invitation? My legs are already spread wide for you."

"Vixen..." he says. "Total vixen," he repeats before lowering back down. He pushes the fabric aside, exposing my wet pussy to him. I practically come off the bed when he blows on my skin. The coolness mixed with the wetness sends me spiraling.

"Lee!" I screech his name. My hands find his hair, and I sink them into it and tug him closer. The tip of his nose grazes my clit, and I can already feel it pounding in sync with my heartbeat.

"Hmm..." He hums as he breathes in my pussy that I've pulled into his face. If I wasn't so turned on right now, I might be embarrassed about doing that. Before I know what's happening, he latches his lips around my clit and sucks hard—really fucking hard. I don't even register the two fingers sliding inside me, at first. All I register is the tongue flicking against the bundle of nerves and the waves of plea-sure wreaking havoc on my body. I don't think I've ever come this hard, and we haven't even had sex yet. This is all from some kissing and a little oral sex.

When my body collapses on the bed, he releases my clit and smiles up at me. I don't even know how I register that is what's happening, but I do.

Lee slides up the bed, lying next to me as my body basks in the afterglow of an orgasm.

"That was incredible," I tell him once I've recov-ered some.

"I'd have to agree." He chuckles.

I shift a little closer to him, resting my head on his chest. I can't help it; my eyes slide shut as I'm in his arms, our bodies touching the entire length of my body.

"I'm ready for more when you are," I tell him. I don't want to accidentally fall asleep now that I'm very relaxed.

"Let's go take a shower," he suggests. I'm a little confused by the request.

"But we haven't gotten dirty yet," I pout, pushing up so I can look at him.

He leans forward, catching my lip with his teeth. "Don't worry, sweetheart, I plan on making you *very* dirty in the shower, and then again when we're out here."

"In that case..." I tell him as I pop up. Once I'm on my feet, I slide my panties down my legs, kicking them to the side once they're down to my ankles.

I grab Lee's hand and tug him up and toward the bathroom.

He pulls out two clean towels from the small closet, setting them on the counter before he reaches into the shower and turns on the water.

"It just takes a minute for it to fully warm-up," he says, leaning in to press his lips to mine. I can taste myself on his lips.

He places a hand under the water, testing the temperature, before holding a hand out for me to step in first. "Get comfortable; I'll be in with you in just a second. I need to grab a condom," he says before darting out of the bathroom.

I step under the hot spray, my muscles instantly relaxing more from the heat. It doesn't take long before Lee's stepping in behind me. He sets the foil packet down on the shelf next to his body wash, then wraps his hands around my torso, pulling my back flush with his front. I can't miss the hard cock that is pressed against my backside. I've still yet to see it with my own eyes, but if it looks anything like it feels, I'm not sure how I'll be walking tomorrow.

"You have the best rack I've ever touched," Lee says as he cups my breasts. "Perfect size," he says, giving them a gentle squeeze. "Pert nipples I could suck on all day and never tire," plucking at them, causing them to harden.

He slides a hand down until he's cupping my sex. "But they don't have anything on this pussy. I could definitely eat this for every meal." He circles my clit with his fingers before dipping them lower and into my entrance.

"Fuck, Lee," I whimper.

"You want my cock, sweetheart?" he growls into my ear.

"Yes," I say, nodding my head, so he doesn't miss it at all.

"What the lady asks for, she shall receive," he says, spinning me around to face him. I instantly reach for his cock, stroking my hands up and down the hard shaft. He's got an impressive erection. Long and thick, but not so thick I think he'll break me or not fit.

"I don't know what I want more, your cock inside my mouth or pussy," I tell him, looking up at him for the first time since facing one another.

"If you drop to your knees now, there's no way I'll last until I'm inside your pussy, and I don't want to come down your throat the first time we're together," he says, and reaches for the condom.

I take the foil packet from his hands, ripping it open with my teeth. I remove it from the package and roll it down his shaft.

"You ready for me, sweetheart?" he asks as he backs me up against the wall. The water has slashed against it, thankfully heating the tiles up slightly.

"I was born ready," I tell him. He lines his tip up with my entrance, and before I can suck in a breath, he's thrust fully inside me. My body screams at the intrusion. The immense amount of pleasure this one thrust has already flooding through my body is almost embarrassing.

"Fuck, Allison. You're so tight." He pants into my neck as he starts at a frantic pace. Our bodies mold together as he holds me tightly against the shower wall. I never once worry that he'll drop me. The way he caresses my body makes me believe that it is precious—*I'm* precious—to him.

"Play with your clit; I need you there," he says, and I slide a hand between our bodies as instructed, finding my clit and pressing down on it. It doesn't take long before I can feel my body start to crest over the orgasm ledge. I take Lee with me, his body slamming into mine one last time. I can feel how shaky his legs are as they hold both of us up after such a strong release.

He lifts his head, his lips finding mine in a languid kiss. It is over before I wanted it to be, but I realize he's still holding me up; his cock is still buried deep inside me, still pulsing with his orgasm.

"I'm going to need some time to rebound from that," he says as he pulls out, stepping back slightly so he can set me back down on my feet.

"After a performance like that, I don't blame you."

"Don't worry, I still have plans for you tonight," he says, slapping my wet ass.

We both rinse off quickly before turning the water off and stepping out of the shower. He wraps me up in one of the fluffy towels he set out, then slings the other one around his own waist.

"Need anything from the kitchen?" he asks as we make our way out to the bedroom.

"Um, maybe," I state.

"I definitely need some nourishment," he says and walks down the hall. I find his T-shirt and pull it on, then go to find him.

He's pulling out some summer sausage, cheese,

and crackers by the time I make it to him. I hop up on his counter and watch as he slices the sausage, laying it out on a plate along with cut up cheese. It might not be fancy, but it is perfect.

He sets down the knife, then comes to stand in front of me. "This looks better on you than it does on me," he says, tugging at his shirt before he slips his hand under the bottom of it that rests high on my thighs. I make sure to keep my legs together so I don't flash him, but it is pointless as he quickly realizes I'm naked underneath.

"Woman, you're going to kill me before the night is over."

"What?" I question, trying my hardest to feign my innocence.

"Like I said earlier. You're a vixen." He kisses me chastely before stepping back over to the cutting board and finishing up what he was working on.

"Want a beer?" he asks as he steps back to the fridge, putting away the food he didn't cut up and pulling out a beer for himself.

"Sure," I say, taking the bottle from him.

He grabs the plate and his beer and heads back for the bedroom.

"Come join me," he says, patting the bed. I sit on it, sliding toward the center where he's already sitting up. The towel he had wrapped around his hips is gaping open, hardly covering his cock. The one that is already rebounding, if the tent that's starting to pitch indicates what's to come.

I take a slice of sausage, cheese, and a cracker, making a little sandwich of the three. I didn't realize I was so hungry until the first bite hits my tongue.

We quickly eat our midnight snack, then Lee moves the plate to the end table once the last of it is gone. We both slide down the bed until we're lying next to each other, my head back on his chest, and his arm is around my body. His fingertips draw random things on my back and side.

"Can I tell you something?" he asks out of the blue.

"Of course, you can tell me anything," I tell him.

"Watching you out on the dance floor tonight drove me fucking wild. Every time you dipped down, I envisioned you doing that on my cock. Every time you swayed your hips back and forth, I envisioned you grinding against me," he says.

"Then why didn't you come dance with me? I would have gladly had you behind me, your hands on my body."

"Because then people would get the wrong idea."

"What do you mean by that?" I question.

"I'm a one-night kind of guy, Allison. You know that. If I was dancing all up on you, it would get people talking and thinking about something else."

"God forbid people think you could settle down." I scoff.

"You know that isn't me," he says.

"If you say so," I tell him, and I can feel a small crack in my heart form. I know the worst thing a girl can do is think she'll be the one to change the proclaimed bachelor, but that is precisely what my traitorous heart and mind have gone and done. I shake it off, not wanting to ruin this night. If I've only got one night with him, I'm damn sure going to make the most of it.

7

ALLISON

"You've got some dishing to do," Lindsay calls out as I walk through her door. I texted her earlier to make sure she'd be home before I dropped by with some wine. I knew she'd want to know what happened last night, and if I'm being honest, I need to talk it out with my best friend.

"Food and wine, and then I'll dish," I tell her before I take the bags I brought straight to the kitchen. She helps me get everything unpacked, as I brought all the fixings for a charcuterie board. Lindsay pulls her board out, and she starts assembling the meat, cheese, and crackers on it while I pull out the wine opener and crack the bottle open, pouring both of us a healthy glass.

"Okay, so..." I finally break my silence as we make our way into the living room. Lindsay carries the board while I have our glasses and two plates. Lindsay sets the board down on the coffee table and takes one of the plates and glasses from my hands. "It was a crazy night. I lost count of how many times we did it," I finally tell her.

"So, it was good, then?" she asks, a smirk on her lips.

"Um, yeah. That boy, I mean, *man* knows how to work it. He was, ahem, *very talented,* to say the least," I dish.

"Good for you. Way to work it. So, was it a one-night kind of hook-up, or are y'all going to do it again?" she asks.

"We didn't define anything, just left it kind of open-ended," I tell her as I shrug my shoulders slightly. We both fill our plates and sit back on the couch, turned so we're facing one another. "Last night, or maybe it was early this morning, I don't really remember what time it was, but anyway, we'd had a little snack because we were both starving. We'd just finished and were just snuggled up together, and he told me what it was like for him to watch me out on the dance floor. How it drove him wild. I asked if that was the case, why he never came out and danced with me. He chalked it up to not wanting to make the wrong impression with all our friends there. He reminded me he is a one-night stand kind of guy, which kind of stung. But then, this morning, he actually asked me if we could do it again, so I have no freaking idea what to really think," I word vomit all over her.

"Did you get *any* sleep?" she prods before taking a sip of her wine.

"Nope," I say, popping the p. "Well, not until I went home. I shit you not, we probably had sex ten times, and he fucking came every time and made me come. As I said, that man is fucking talented in the bedroom."

"Sounds like a fun night." She bounces her eyebrows at me. "Glad it was mutually satisfying."

"I'll be thinking about it for a long time, that's for sure. I also don't know how I'm walking today," I say, laughing.

"So, from the sounds of it, he wants a friends with benefits situation? Are you game for that?" she asks.

"I think so, maybe for a little while. I mean, the sex was phenomenal. I'd be a fool to pass that up."

"Sex isn't everything. I don't want to see you get hurt," Lindsay says.

"I know, and if we do end up with an FWB, I'll go into it with a completely open mind and hopefully not develop any feelings past the attraction I already have for him."

"That's a good plan; I just don't want to see you get hurt. FWB situations tend to never work out, someone always catches feelings, and they end up broken-hearted and lose a friendship, as well."

"I know, but what if he changes his mind. What if he realizes that what we have is real and he wants to give it a shot?" I question.

"Then you ride off into the sunset madly in love, but you might also be drowning your sorrows in wine while eating your weight in ice cream."

"I know. Being an adult sucks," I say, downing the rest of my wine.

"Oh, before I forget, I ran into Tucker at the grocery store today, and he invited both of us to a football and bonfire party next Saturday. I told him that I wasn't sure if I could make it since I told Betty I'd cover her shift if she needed me to."

"Sounds like fun," I tell her; I don't know that I'd show up for the football portion, but a bonfire sounds fun.

"Tucker said Lee will be there."

"I figured that." I laugh. "Those boys don't do much without one another. Kinda like us," I quip.

"Yep," she agrees with me before we fall into a fit of giggles.

8

LEE

Are you off today?

ALLISON

I am; what's up?

Lunch?

Are you asking me out on a date?

Can't friends grab lunch together?

Of course they can; I was just trying to determine what kind of lunch this was. If it is just two friends grabbing food together, I can meet you in ten, but if it's a date, I'll need an hour to shower and get dressed.

> No need to get dressed up for me, sweetheart. To be honest, I'd rather just strip your clothes off of you and feast on you.

> Such a charmer.

> You know you like it. {winky face}

> {eye roll}

> So that's a yes to lunch?

> Sure, when and where?

> The deli in fifteen?

> Okay, see you then.

I SLIDE MY PHONE INTO MY POCKET, LAUGHING AND shaking my head at my text conversation with Allison. I'd be lying if I said I didn't love her sassy attitude. She isn't afraid to put me into my place or call me on my bullshit. I've never been with a woman who was like that. Maybe that is what was always missing with the few women I've attempted to date.

I snag my keys off the hook and head for my truck. It's been almost a week since she left my bed after the best night ever. We fucked like rabbits that night, neither one of us seeming to get enough of the other. I've had some wild nights before, but that one took the top spot. Hopefully, we'll have a repeat of it sooner than later.

The idea of more with Allison has my head spinning. I don't usually think like that when it comes to women, but she has me thinking all sorts of things that I wouldn't usually think about.

I crank up the volume of the radio once I'm in my truck. An old Garth Brooks song is playing, one I loved growing up, so I blast it as I sing at the top of my lungs while I make it the few miles to the deli I'm meeting Allison at.

It doesn't take me long to find a parking spot. Small town living and all that, plus, it isn't quite noon yet, so the rush hasn't started.

I head inside and grab a small table along the wall of windows. It won't take long for this place to fill up once the noon hour hits, so snagging a place for us to eat will come in handy.

I scan over the specials menu, picking out what I want while waiting for Allison to get here. Each time the bells above the door chime, alerting everyone that someone new is walking in, I look towards the door in search of her. A few people trickle in, heading straight for the counter to place their orders before taking seats.

I pull my phone out, playing one of the many

games I have downloaded for moments like this when I'm bored and passing time. I look up when the door chimes and can't help but smile when I see Allison come walking in. She's in an oversized sweat-shirt, leggings, and some boots. My mouth waters as I drink her in. As she gets closer to me, I'm able to take in more details. She's got her hair up in a messy bun, and it doesn't look like she's got a stitch of makeup on. If I could pick the way she looked all the time, this is the exact look I'd go for.

"Hey," she says, waving a little awkwardly as she stops next to me.

"Hey, yourself. Glad you could make it. Want to head up and order?" I ask, standing from my seat.

I place my hand on the small of her back as we walk up to the counter. We both quickly place our orders and head back to the table to wait for our number to be called.

"How's your week been?" she asks once we're sitting.

"Pretty good; I got off yesterday. Went home and crashed after that shift. It was a brutal one with little sleep."

"Sorry to hear that. What happened? I didn't hear about anything major going on."

"Nothing major, just a lot of little calls that kept coming in."

"Ah, so just not much time to sleep between calls then."

"Nope. I think the longest we had all night was an hour between calls. It was brutal."

"I can't imagine that. My days are long in the ER, but at least I get to go home after twelve hours. I don't know how y'all do it with working twenty-fours."

"It can be challenging at times, but then, there'll be days we sit around all shift and don't get anything."

"Does that happen often?" she asks.

"No, we usually get at least a few calls every shift. Sometimes they're minor, like an old woman with her cat stuck in the tree—"

"Wait a minute, you actually get those kinds of calls? That isn't just a metaphor people use?" she says with a laugh.

"Not a metaphor. I've rescued my fair share of kittens over the years," I tell her just as our order number is called. I stand to grab the tray, stopping at the counter to get us some napkins and silverware.

I set it down on our table, removing my items

from the tray as Allison does the same. Once it is empty, we get to work eating it all.

We eat in companionable silence. I'm not sure if it's just me, or the both of us, but I can feel something crackling between us. I know from my end it is a sexual pull. I want nothing more than to take this woman back to my place and strip her bare.

"What are you thinking about or contemplating?" Allison asks as she sets down her half-eaten club sandwich.

"What makes you think I was contemplating something?" I retort.

"Because you keep furrowing your brow and have pushed the same five fries around your plate for the last five minutes," she says, and I look down and realize I'm doing exactly that.

"You've got me there," I state. "Honestly?" I say, but it comes out more like a question.

"I only ever want the God's honest truth from you," she says.

"I've been thinking about you constantly since you left my place the other morning. Not just in the mornings or when I'm lying in bed wishing that you were wrapped up in my sheets still, but all fucking day and night. It's like you've sunk your way into my subconscious, and I can't get you off my mind."

"I don't really know what to say to that."

"I can't offer you anything more than sex right now. We both know how good that is, so why not explore that a little more?" I suggest, hoping like hell she'll accept my half-assed proposal.

"So, just sex?" she questions.

"Yes."

"Exclusive?"

"If I have my way with things, you won't have time for any other man." I smirk. "But if it would make you feel better about things, I can agree to those terms. No one else. If either one of us wants someone else, then we end our little agreement and move on with our lives."

"Okay," she agrees, and I think my chin about hits the tabletop. I didn't believe that it would be quite this easy, but I'll be damned, it was.

"What are you doing after lunch?" I ask.

"You," she states. My cock swells so fast in my jeans that I'm not sure I'll be able to stand and walk out of here.

"Fuck yes, you will be," I finally choke out.

She flashes me a fiery look that has my blood boiling and a desire to sink balls deep into her as soon as possible.

9

ALLISON

I FOLLOW LEE OUT TO THE PARKING LOT. I WAS ABLE to park right next to his truck.

"Your place or mine?" he asks.

"I don't care," I tell him.

"Mine's closer, so I'll follow you there," he says.

I unlock my car and slide into the driver's seat. I still can't believe we meet up like this and end our meet-ups with a roll in the sheets. Don't get me wrong, the sex is life-changing, but it still sometimes feels a little strange.

I drive the few miles to Lee's place, hitting the two lights green, so nothing slows us down. My body is already humming at the knowledge of what's to come. I swear, this man can turn me on with just one smoldering look from across the room.

I pull into his driveway and park to the side, allowing him to pull into his main spot. I cut the engine but wait a minute to take a few deep and calming breaths. When I open my eyes back up, Lee's standing next to my driver's side door.

I open the door and swing my legs to the side so I can step out.

"Everything okay?" he asks, the concern furrowing his brow.

"Yeah, just needed a minute," I tell him honestly.

"You sure?" he pushes.

"Yes," I assure him. I stand to my full height, still nowhere near his height, seeing as how I just reach his shoulder. I dig deep, find some confidence that I don't always have, push up on my toes, and plant a chaste kiss on his lips.

He wraps his hands around my torso, pulling me in closer as he deepens the kiss. What I'd intended to be a quick peck, he's turning into a full-on make-out session.

He breaks our kiss, resting his forehead against mine for a few seconds. "Let's get inside; we can get a little more comfortable."

I follow Lee inside his house, kicking off my shoes once inside his front door.

He closes the door behind us. I startle when his

hands slide along my sides, coming to rest on my abdomen. His lips find my neck as he moves my hair off my shoulders to give him better access. "Do you need anything before I strip you and have my wicked way with you?" he says against my skin.

"No," I manage to say. Lee's lips against my skin are very distracting and turn me on.

"Good." He smirks before sucking on my neck. He starts to walk us toward the bedroom, tugging at our clothes as we move that way. By the time we reach his doorway, he's got my shirt up and pulls it over my head. His hands cup my breasts, and I love the stimulation him rolling my nipples provides. My center clenches, and I can feel my desire as it dampens my panties. "Fuck," he grits out when one of his hands slips down and finds me wet and ready for him.

He circles my clit before sinking two fingers inside my pussy. My body clenches around him, almost ready to release at the intrusion. He knows just how to strum my body to life, playing me like a professional musician would play their instrument of choice.

"Lee," I moan his name. "I'm going to come," I warn him. "Don't stop; I'm so close!" I cry out.

"Fuck yes, you are," he says as he spins me

around, so I'm now facing him. He backs me against the wall, all while never slowing his hand from fucking me. He kisses me hard while working his own jeans open and down his hips.

I whimper at the loss of his fingers. My eyes open, and I look down to see why in the hell he stopped. I find him sheathing his engorged cock in a condom. Before I can say anything, he's lining up with my entrance and thrusting in, hard and fast.

My body instantly stretches to accommodate him. He's so fucking deep at this angle and position.

"Holy shit, Allison," he grits as he pounds into me; his rhythm is fast and unrelenting. "I swear your pussy was made for me," he says as he brings his lips to mine in a punishing kiss.

I bite at his bottom lip. My body practically floats as I climb higher and higher toward my orgasm.

"You like that?" he asks as he rotates his hips slightly after pulling out. The way it causes his pelvic bone to tap into my clit has me seeing stars as I fall over the edge, my orgasm taking over. Lee thrusts a few more times, his own body cresting over the edge as we come together.

He slows his thrusts, holding me against the wall. It's then I realize we never fully got undressed. My pants are still around one leg, my bra is still in place. Lee's pants and boxers are around his ankles. He must have pulled his shirt off when he pulled mine, as it is on the floor with it.

"Wow," I finally say, looking up at him.

"I swear, against the wall sex with you is the best there is." He smirks, placing a chaste kiss against my lips.

"We never seem to make it to a bed for the first time, do we?" I muse.

"We're explosive like that," he adds.

"Nothing wrong with being explosive," I tell him as he finally slips out of me and sets me back down on the floor. I take my pants and panties all the way off, fixing them so they're ready for me when it's time to get dressed again later.

10

LEE

I STROLL OUT THE BACK DOOR OF MY BEST FRIEND Tucker's house. We just finished watching the Georgia/Alabama game. With the game over, the party is starting to make its way outside. He's got a bonfire area, as well as a small pond on his land.

I head for the bonfire pile. I might be a firefighter and get paid to put fires out, but lighting shit on fire is just as fun as putting those fires out. Firefighters are nothing but pyro enthusiasts in disguise.

"You coming?" I shout at Tucker. He's standing in the back doorway with Lindsay, the only woman I've known him to get tripped up over.

"Hold your horses, we're coming," Lindsay calls out to me as she turns into Tucker. I wave them off and keep heading toward the fire pile. I don't give it long before they're a couple, especially with how he held her close during the game.

I open the bottle of lighter fluid, making my way around the pile as I soak the wood in the liquid. I want this fire to be big tonight. There's not much better than sitting around a fire after dark on a crisp fall evening. Add in a few beautiful women, some music, a drink or two, and good conversation, and it's my ideal night off.

I get the fire going, making sure it isn't going to jump from the pile; I don't need to light anything else in Tucker's backyard on fire. He'd kill me if that happened. He's worked hard to make this land his home over the last few years, making it a place that he can call home with his daughter, and if my suspicions are correct, maybe even Lindsay in the future.

"Hey," I hear a sweet voice call out from behind me. Turning, I see it is Allison. We've been "seeing" each other for the last week. I'm not the kind of guy looking to settle down, or the looking for forever kind of guy. I like to fuck, and I'm not shy about that fact. There's something about this woman, though, she has a pull that draws me closer. Has ever since we were kids.

"Hey, sweetheart. You made it," I drawl, emphasizing my southern accent.

"Yeah, football isn't really my thing," she says, scrunching her nose up.

"I know." I smirk as I slip a finger through the belt loop on her skintight jeans and pull her closer until she's inches away from me. "How was your day?" I ask, sliding my hand around her hip and holding her close. I suck in a breath, taking in her sweet shampoo or perfume and enjoying it a hell of a lot better than the lighter fluid I just sprayed over the fire pit.

"Good, just a lazy Saturday."

"Nothing wrong with that; you deserve to take some time for yourself," I tell her, brushing some loose strands of hair back and tucking them behind her ear. "Want something to eat or drink? I think there's still plenty of food."

"I ate before I came, but I'll take a beer if there's an extra one around."

"Of course, make yourself comfortable around the fire, and I'll be right back." I release Allison as I step back and take off for the deck. I snag two beers from one of the coolers and jog my way back.

I find her sitting on one of the logs, the flicker of the fire lighting up her features as the sun has now set. I hear music strike up from the deck; Tucker must have turned on his outside system. I sit on the log next to Allison, popping the top of both beers and handing her one. We clink bottles before taking our first sips.

"Thanks," Allison says, her head resting against my shoulder as we both sit facing the fire.

"Anytime," I tell her, taking another swig of my beer. "What's on your mind? You seem a little quiet tonight."

"Nothing, just been a busy week, and I'm exhausted. I almost didn't come tonight, but I knew if I didn't at least show up for a few minutes, Lindsay would be mad."

"I'm glad you're here," I tell her as I wrap an arm around her shoulder and hold her against me. I might say I don't want more with someone, but Allison has had me thinking otherwise lately. The quick fuck, or night rolling in the sheets and then her sneaking out come morning is starting to get old.

Lindsay makes her way over and sits down next to us. She straddles the log, facing us rather than the fire.

"Did you finish painting today?" Lindsay asks Allison. She pops her head off my shoulder and shifts to mirror Lindsay on the log.

"I didn't even attempt to. I just bummed around. Curled up with a good book and read for a few hours. The only productive thing I did today was clean my bathroom, then took a long-ass bath and finished my book."

"Sounds like the perfect day. Maybe I can come over later this week and help you finish up with the painting," Lindsay offers.

"I'll take you up on that," Allison says before tipping her head back and taking a long drink from her beer bottle. I follow suit and shift so that I'm straddling the log, my legs going around Allison's. I slip a hand along her waist, my fingertips finding bare skin where her shirt has ridden up. It's been a few nights since we were last together, and I find myself itching to get her back to my place and these clothes stripped off both of us.

I sit back, allowing the two women to have their own conversation, adding things now and again. I look around, the crowd has thinned out as the evening has gone on. Tucker finally joins us, and he slides in behind Lindsay on the log, mirroring my stance. The way he was all over Lindsay tonight makes me think that things are brewing between the two of them, and it's just a matter of time before he'll be a taken man.

"Ready to get out of here?" I ask Allison when there's a lull in the conversation.

"Sure," she agrees, a yawn hitting her.

I stand up, then offer her my hand to help her up. I might be a one-night stand kind of guy, but I'm still a goddamn southern gentleman who has manners and knows how to use them.

I lead Allison out to my truck and realize that Tucker is also escorting Lindsay to her car. "Night, guys," I call out to Lindsay and Tucker as I go to open the passenger door of my truck for Allison.

"I'll just follow you so that I have my car," Allison says, stepping up into my space. She drops a kiss on my cheek, then steps around me and heads for her car. I quickly close the door, then jog over to her car so that I can open the door for her. *Those manners are coming out again.*

"See you in a few," she says, sliding into the driver's seat. I wait until she's clicked the seat belt across her body before I let the door close. As soon as it is secure, I jog back over to my truck and follow her out of the driveway and down the road to my place.

11

ALLISON

I pull into Lee's driveway. This routine is becoming second nature. I don't know why he insists he doesn't do anything more than friends with benefits. He's such an amazing guy, one that I've known for my entire life and have crushed on for years. If he'd just give things a try, I know we could be more, but he's been firm in his position of no strings. No forever. No labels. So, for now, I deal with it.

"I've wanted to strip you out of these clothes since I laid eyes on you tonight," Lee growls in my ear as we make it through his garage door. As soon as the door snicks shut, he pushes me up against it, and his lips land on mine. I let my hands roam over his ripped torso, up and over his strong, broad shoulders, until my fingers slide into the long strands of hair at the nape of his neck. I revel at the way he moans as my fingernails scrape against his scalp as he does naughty things to my mouth with his own. "Fuck," he growls against my lips. "I love it when you do that," he says before lifting me up.

My legs go around his waist. I can feel the bulge his cock is making pressed against my center as he carries me down the hall and into his room. He carefully sets me down on the bed, caging me in as I fall back into it.

"Are you just going to stare at me, or are you going to fuck me?" I toss out, knowing that he's damn well going to fuck me.

"Don't you worry one bit, sweetheart. I'll fuck you so good tonight; you won't be walking tomorrow."

"That's one hell of a promise," I quip back just before he flips the button on my jeans, lowers the zipper, and has them off my body in a few seconds flat.

"A promise I plan to keep," he says just as his hot mouth descends on my center. He pushes my thong to the side, exposing my wet center to his waiting tongue. He wastes no time, sucking my clit between his lips like a starved man, and I'm his only meal in a month.

I thrash as pleasure starts to course its way

through my body. Lee adds two fingers, and my pussy clenches around them. His tongue never stops lashing at my clit, the bundle of nerves almost to the point of being oversensitive as I lose control in a wave of ecstasy.

"That's one," Lee comments as I come down from my orgasm. His head is resting against my inner thigh as he looks up at me. I can see the smirk on his lips; he's obviously proud of himself for bringing me to orgasm so quickly.

"And how many are you going to give me tonight?" I ask, my eyebrows disappearing into my hairline, I'm sure.

"As many as I can." He bounces his own eyebrows at me as he slides up my body.

"I think you're a little overdressed, then," I quip.

"I can fix that, sweetheart." He pushes off the bed and strips out of his jeans, T-shirt, and boxers. "Now who's overdressed?" he asks.

I get lost watching as he strokes his cock, forgetting to answer him or move a muscle of my own. "Allison." His voice pulls me out of my trance.

"Yeah," I attempt to say, having to stop and clear my throat before repeating it.

"Strip, and we can continue." He smirks. I tug my shirt off over my head, then quickly lose my bra and thong. I lay back on the bed, naked now, and turn my full attention back to Lee. I watch his every move as he goes to his nightstand and pulls out a strip of condoms. He tears off one of the packets and tosses it on the bed next to me, then places another two on the nightstand before returning the rest of the strip to the drawer. I snag the packet, tearing it open with my teeth and pulling it out of the package. I crook a finger at him, beckoning him to join me on the bed so that I can sheath his cock. He kneels on the bed, staying up on his knees as he comes next to me.

I lean forward, taking his cock in my mouth. I suck him deep, adding a fist to his shaft as I pull back. I can feel a hand sink into my hair as he helps direct my mouth up and down his cock. I give him a few hard, cheek-hallowing sucks before I pop his dick from my mouth and slide the condom down his length. I give his chest a little shove and demand, "Lay back; I want to be on top."

"Yes, ma'am." He complies. His hands go to my hips as I straddle him. I reach between us and grip his cock so that I can line it up with my entrance. I slowly sink down on him, his size stretching me out as I take in every last inch he's packing.

"Holy shit," I moan, feeling full as I start to move. His shaft is hitting me just right, causing my body to already want to pulse around him, but I hold it off as I find a faster rhythm. The bed is protesting, and we might leave a hole in his wall, but at this moment, I don't care about any of that. All I care about is finding this release.

"That's it, sweetheart," Lee encourages me, his hands having moved from my hips. One is rubbing circles on my clit as the other pinches and tweaks my nipples as we both chase our release.

"I'm coming!" I cry out as my body convulses around his cock. I fall forward, my heart about ready to beat out of my chest as I suck in a lungful of air.

"Fucking-A. I could come in your pussy daily and never get tired of it," Lee calls out as I feel him crest over his own release. I try not to let his words sink in. I know he's just saying things in the moment of pleasure.

I roll off him, snuggling into his side. We might be in this FWB situation, but he's never just kicked me out. He's unlike anyone else I've ever had a fling with. He actually wants to cuddle and talk and spend some time together, so I take what I can get and try not to let the rest get to me.

"WHERE ARE YOU GOING?" LEE'S SLEEP-FILLED VOICE calls out as I slip out of his warm king-size bed.

"I was going to go to the bathroom and then head home," I tell him, turning to look at him over my shoulder.

"Why?" he asks, sitting up.

"Um, because?" I reply, but it comes out more like a question.

"Go to the bathroom, but then come back to bed. I'm not done with you," he states. I watch as he tugs back the covers on his bed. I stall for another second before padding my way into his bathroom to take care of business.

As I wash my hands, I take a good look at my reflection in the mirror. I can see the sadness lingering in the depths of my own eyes. Continuing with this little charade is slowly killing me inside. I know when I walk back out into that room, Lee is going to flash me that smile I can't resist, and I'll slide right back between his sheets instead of pulling my clothes on and going home, where I would drink and cry myself to sleep.

"Hurry up; the sheets are getting cold," Lee calls from the bedroom. I shut the water off, drying my hands on the towel hanging from the hook on the wall.

I step out of the bathroom, still naked. I can feel his eyes roaming over my exposed flesh. My mind and heart are fighting internally as to who is going to win this war.

"What's wrong?" Lee asks, sitting up in bed. The look of concern on his face has my heart melting just a bit.

"Just not feeling all that great. I think I'm going to head home," I tell him, taking a few steps towards where my clothes are strewn around his room. He meets me at the side of the bed, stopping me from pulling my clothes back on as he slides a hand around my waist and pulls me until our bodies are flush against one another.

"You'd tell me if it was something else, if something was bothering you, right?" he asks as if he already knows that something *is* bothering me.

"Yeah," I lie, the words coming out as a whisper. I have to suck in a breath to keep the tears at bay.

"Do you need anything? Some 7-Up and crackers? Soup? Sleep?" he asks, rapid-fire.

"No." I shake my head slightly. "I just need a good night's sleep."

"Then come to bed, let me hold you. I promise no funny business; I'll just hold you all night and let you sleep," he offers.

I suck my bottom lip between my teeth, chewing on it as I ponder what I'm going to do. Get dressed and go home, or allow him to hold me in bed? Once again, my heart and mind are boxing it out. Lee must recognize the raging war inside my mind as he tugs my hand a few feet to the edge of the bed. He slides in, pulling me with him until we're settled. Lee's head is on his pillow, and he's situated me with my head on his chest with his arm around my body, holding me tight. I hold back the tears, his touch soothing, as his hand glides up and down my back.

"I have a question for you," he says, breaking the silence that we've settled into.

"What's that?"

"Would you be my date to the Firefighters Ball?"

I mull his question over, a little shocked that he's asked. "I'd love to," I tell him honestly.

"It's formal, so you'd need a dress and all that," he tells me.

"That isn't a problem. It just gives me a reason to go shopping," I tell him.

His question lifts my mood a little bit. Maybe he is coming around to the idea that we could be more than just fuck buddies. With that thought, and perhaps a little bit of hope, I snuggle in a little tighter to his side and fall asleep.

12

LEE

Allison was up and out of here early this morning. Something was off with her last night, and I really wish I knew what exactly it was. We've got a good thing going between us, but I'm out if things get too weird. I'd rather have her as a friend than have things going sideways.

I hop out of the shower, drying off and wrapping the towel around my waist as I step up in front of my sink and mirror. I start with my electric razor before cleaning the rest of my scruff up with my handheld one and then head into my bedroom to get dressed and ready for my shift. I pack a bag since I'll be at the firehouse for a full twenty-four-hour shift.

"What's up, man?" Tucker asks, strolling into the locker room, his own bag slung over his shoulder. He bumps fists with me before offloading his things into his locker.

"Nothing much, how about you?" I ask him as I shut my locker door and close the few feet between us.

"Just an easy day, spent it with my girl before I had to come to work."

I smirk at him, referring to Lindsay as his girl. Settling down actually suits him.

I kick back in the great room, a random car show on the TV, as the rest of our crew is milling about, waiting for the first call of our shift to come in. It only takes us sitting around for about thirty minutes before the bells are ringing, and we all go running for the rigs in the bays.

We roll up on the house, smoke billowing from the upper windows. I can already tell this is going to be a total loss for this family.

"Ma'am," I call out to the woman standing at the end of the driveway, tears streaming down her face as she looks at the burning house. "Is anyone still inside?" I ask, wanting to know if we need to get in and rescue anyone.

"No," she chokes out between sobs. "I was the only one home. My husband was gone with our kids."

"That's good," I tell her, trying to show her as much sympathy as I can. "Do you know how the fire started?" I ask.

"I think from the dryer, but I really don't know. I was busy cleaning the bathroom when the smoke detector went off," she tells me as some of my crew starts spraying water on the house as others head inside to fight this from both sides. "When I came out of the bathroom, the hallway was already filled with smoke, so I ran out of the house and called you guys."

"You did great, ma'am. We'll get things under control as quickly as we can. Do you need any medical attention? Does it hurt to breathe?" I question. Smoke inhalation can cause damage quickly, so depending on how much smoke she had to go through before making it outside, it could possibly have caused damage to her lungs.

"I don't think so," she answers, her body visibly shaking, most likely from the shock the fire has caused.

We do everything we can to get the fire out, but

as I feared when we rolled up, the house was completely lost. Between the smoke, fire, and water damage, not much inside will be salvageable. By the time we got the flames knocked down, the husband and kids had shown back up. I noticed the man holding his wife as she cried into his shoulder when I walked back to the truck for one of the axes.

We finish up, ensuring we've put out all the smoldering embers everywhere before packing up our equipment and heading back to the station.

***

"WHO'S ON DINNER DUTY TONIGHT?" I ASK THE GROUP as I finish dressing after a quick shower. Fighting fires is not only a dirty job because of the ashes and soot that we end up covered in, but we're a sweaty mess by the time we're done. Turnout gear only protects you from so much.

"I think we're going to order in," Tucker says, flipping through the menu book we keep with all the restaurants' menus, not that any of us really need them to know what we'd want from anywhere. In the last five years or so, we've had more chain places popping up since we're on the interstate, but the really good, hole in the wall, local places are where it's at.

"Good, I'm starving," I tell him as my stomach growls loudly.

"Then you pick," he says, handing over the menu binder.

"Like you even have to ask," I scoff. I always pick our local BBQ place. They've got large servings, are usually super-fast, and best of all, not that far from the station.

"Figured." Tucker laughs and shakes his head at me. "I swear you'd eat there every day if you could."

"What can I say? I like their food."

It doesn't take long before we've got our order called in and back here at the station so we can all dive in. Thankfully, things are on our side tonight as we don't get called out on our next call until well after we've had dinner.

My shift finally ticks by; I swear tonight felt like it was never going to end. Thankfully, I was able to get a decent stretch of sleep, not that I won't still just head home and crash for the next few hours.

I pull into my garage, shutting my truck off before hitting the button on my opener to close the door before I step out of the truck. The sun is bright, and with it no longer shining in, my eyes take a few minutes to adjust to the dimmer room. I snag my bag from the truck seat, slinging it over my shoulder as I head into my house.

I drop everything just inside the door and head straight for my bed. I slide between the sheets, my phone pinging from the nightstand as I do. I grab it to see who's texting me this morning and see I've got a message from Allison. My dick twitches just reading her name, but now's not the time for that appendage to be in charge.

ALLISON

Hey! Are you free tonight? Maybe we can grab a drink?

Her text comes across as her usual bubbly self, so I can only hope that means whatever was bugging her the other night is no longer bothering her.

Sure, I just got home and was going to crash for a few more hours. Did you want to get together this afternoon?

I'm off today, so we can get together whenever.

How about I text you when I'm up and moving for the day?

Works for me; enjoy your nap.
{winky face}

I toss my phone aside once again, doing my best to shut my mind off long enough to fall asleep for a few more hours.

13

———

ALLISON

Two months later

I STAND IN FRONT OF THE MIRROR, CHECKING OVER MY complete look for tonight. I splurged and had my hair and makeup done at the salon today. I love the way my hair is styled, and my makeup is on point.

"Lee is going to swallow his tongue when he sees you, girl!" Lindsay says. She's going with Tucker to the ball tonight, so we did the salon thing together.

"Just like Tucker will with you," I tell my best friend.

"I guess we're some pretty lucky women. Have some amazing guys escorting us tonight that we both know are a sure thing later." She smirks.

I love my best friend, and she knows the score

between Lee and me, but her words cut deep. She might have the sweetest man who's swept her off her feet, but that isn't the same for me. Lee and I are just fuck buddies. I'd love to be more, but I'm afraid to tell him that. I'm worried that he'll tell me he can't do anything more and then cut me out of his life.

"What's wrong?" Lindsay asks, noticing that I've gone quiet.

I shake off her comment; I don't want to cry and mess up my makeup for tonight. "It's nothing," I tell her, straightening my spine and plastering on a fake smile. I know she can see right through me, but she must see something in my expression because she somewhat lets it go.

"I know something is bothering you; if I let it go for now, will you tell me later?"

"Yes, I promise. I just don't want to cry before the guys get here."

"Okay, tomorrow we're having a girls' day," she states.

"Sounds perfect." I hug Lindsay. She's genuinely the sister I never had growing up. I don't know what I'd do without her in my life. We've been by each other's side for so long that I can't even remember a time before we were friends.

Lee holds his hand out for me to take as I exit the limo. The guys splurged and hired it for tonight. That way, none of us had to drive, especially since the ball has an open bar.

"Thank you." I smile up at him as I stand on my high heels. The moment I saw these in the store, I just knew I had to have them. I also knew they'd drive him crazy.

"You look fucking incredible tonight," Lee whispers into my ear once I'm standing in front of him. "If it wasn't for Tucker and Lindsay being with us, I wouldn't have let you out of your place."

"No way, mister. I didn't spend all day getting ready for tonight for you not to take me out. I'm getting everything out of this fancy party."

"All right, then. Let's go," he says and takes my hand, slipping it in the crook of his elbow as he escorts me into the hotel.

We quickly find the ballroom the event is being held in. It is simple but elegant. A large dance floor in the middle of the room is surrounded by large round tables and chairs.

We find a table with other guys from their firehouse, the four of us fill in the remaining empty seats. It isn't long before the fire commissioner takes command of the room from the podium in the center of a stage behind the dance floor.

After his welcome speech, the servers start making their rounds with our dinner. The department goes all out on this ball, from what I can tell. The food is top-notch, and the alcohol is flowing.

"Care to join me out on the dance floor?" Lee asks once we've finished our dinner and the music has started to play.

"I'd love to, Mr. Crawford," I tell him, accepting his hand. He's always got a sexy vibe, but he is sex on legs in his dress uniform tonight.

Lee leads me out onto the dance floor, then pulls me in close to his body as a slow song plays over the speaker. "Are you having a good time tonight?" he asks after a few moments.

"I am, are you?" I ask. I shift so I can look up at him as we dance and talk.

"Yes, although, I still can't wait to get you home and out of this dress. It looks fan-fucking-tastic on you, but it will look even better on my bedroom floor."

"You're incorrigible." I laugh at him and shake my head. I swear he'd spend his entire life in bed if he had things his way.

"I'm just incredibly attracted to the sexy woman in my arms. Can't blame a man for wanting to keep her locked in his bed forever." I suck in a quick breath at his words. I know he doesn't really mean those in the sense that I'd like him to.

I rest my head against his chest again, enjoying the feeling of our bodies being pressed against one another.

Before long, the DJ turns up the tempo on the music, busting out the songs that have everyone up and off their feet and having a good time. I have no idea how much time passes; I just know that we have the best night, dancing and drinking with our friends until the last call comes and the DJ closes the night out with one last slow song for all the couples left in the room. Tucker and Lindsay hold each other tight as they sway around the floor; I envy their new relationship. They both have gone all-in with seeing where things go between them, and I am cheering them on the entire way.

"I can't believe we closed the party down!" Lindsay says once we're all piled back in the limo.

"That was definitely the best ball I've been to," Tucker says, tugging Lindsay closer so he can kiss her.

"That's because you finally had a date," Lee teases him.

"Maybe," Tucker replies.

I think the exhaustion of the night finally starts to settle in as we all relax back into the comfortable seats as the limo driver takes us home. He stops first at Lee's place, dropping the two of us off before continuing on to take Lindsay and Tucker to his place.

"Finally, I've got you to myself," Lee growls as he lets me inside.

I stifle a yawn, exhaustion hitting me hard after the long evening. "You sure do," I tell him as we both make our way into the house.

I beeline it for his couch. As much as I love these heels, they have got to go now. My feet are killing me after dancing for hours in them. "Oh my god," I moan once my feet are free.

"Are you having fun without me?" Lee asks, coming back into the room with two glasses of water.

"No, my feet were killing me in my shoes," I tell him. He hands me one of the glasses, then sets the other down on the end table. He takes a seat and pulls my feet into his lap. My head falls back on the cushion, and a moan falls from my lips when he starts massaging my feet.

"Is this turning you on?" Lee asks. I crack my eyes open to look at him.

"It just might," I tell him as he digs his knuckles into my arch, and I can't help but moan again. "Fuck, that feels amazing."

"I know something else that will feel amazing." He chuckles.

"I'm sure you do," I say, my eyes closed again while I enjoy his hands massaging my tired feet.

"All right, sweetheart, you're falling asleep on my couch. Let's get you out of this dress and into bed," Lee quietly says. I must have dozed off for a few minutes. He picks me up into his arms, cradling me close as he carries me to his bedroom.

"You can put me down; I can walk," I tell him once we're inside. He slides me down; I'm pretty sure the way he turns my body is so I feel every ridge of his hardness as I do so.

He's hard *everywhere*. His cock is hard and thick, tenting his slacks. "You look like you could use some help with this," I say as I cup his erection through his clothing.

"If you're awake enough, I'm not going to tell you no."

"I'm sure you can convince me to stay awake for a little while longer." I smile up at him. Without my heels on still, I have to crane my neck to look up at him with us this close together.

"If I have to convince you, then I'm not doing things correctly. You should know by now that I'll make it well worth your while." He winks, and his cocky demeanor slips out.

"That's more like it," I tell him. I still have my hand gripped around his cock, stroking it through his slacks. I release it, taking matters into my own hands. I unbuckle his belt and unzip his pants. I push the elastic of his briefs out of my way so I can grip his cock. I release it from the confines of his briefs and slacks as I drop to my knees. I take him into my mouth. The contrast between his velvety soft skin and rock-hard dick has my body strumming in anticipation of what's to come later when he's inside me with that monster cock.

"God damn, sweetheart," he grits as he slides his hands into my hair. He guides my mouth back and forth as I suck his cock. I reach up, playing with his balls in one hand, using the other to wrap around his base. "Fucking suck that cock," he says. My center floods with moisture as he dirty talks me through the blowjob. Before I can make him finish, he's pulling me up and kissing me hard. "I want you naked and in my bed, now," he commands.

I spin around, exposing my back to him. "I need you to unzip me, please," I tell him when he gives me a zoned-out stare.

He finds the top of the zipper and pulls it down. I love watching the expression change as more of my skin is exposed to him the lower the zipper goes. Once he's reached the bottom, I shimmy my shoulders until the top falls down, and I'm able to push it the rest of the way off my body. I step out of the dress and then to his dresser, where I lay it across the top. The last thing I want to do is ruin my brand new expensive dress by flinging it on the floor in a crumpled mess.

I walk back over to him in nothing but my bra and matching thong set--also new for tonight.

"You are a vision," he says, pulling me back into his arms.

"You're not so bad yourself," I tell him.

He backs me up to the edge of his bed, following me down as I fall backward.

He takes advantage of our positioning and starts kissing my exposed skin from my collar bone; he slowly makes his way down over the tops of my breasts until he removes my bra, giving him full access to my hardening nipples.

"You're so responsive to me tonight," he says into my skin as it puckers under his lips.

"Because you're making me that way," I tell him as he drops lower down my abdomen. When he reaches the edge of the lacy thong, he runs a fingertip over the fabric. My clit throbs at his touch.

"Yes, more," I whimper.

"You want me here?" he asks, circling the nub again before blowing on it. Even with a scrap of fabric between us still, I can feel the air hit me. My body aches for this man to be inside me. To make me feel like I'm floating on cloud nine.

"Yes." I finally answered his question, the one that I didn't even comprehend he was asking.

He lowers his head further, sliding the fabric to the side so he can lick up my slit and around my clit. My back arches off the bed in anticipation and need.

"Easy." He chuckles and places his arm across my hips to hold me down to the bed before he goes back in, sucking my clit into his mouth as he slides two fingers inside me, pumping with a mission. It doesn't take long for that mission to turn into my coming on his tongue and calling out his name as I do so.

14

ALLISON

One week later

I PACE AROUND MY LIVING ROOM AS I WAIT FOR LEE TO arrive. He texted me ten minutes ago, saying that he was up and ready to get together. I've been rehearsing what I'm going to tell him all day. I need to lay all my cards on the table, so to speak, and let them fall where they're going to fall. Our friends with benefits agreement has been going on for months now, but I can't do this anymore. I need more. I've started to fall in love with Lee, and I need him to know.

I know I'm about to blow up what we've had going on, but my heart can't take it anymore. I see how happy my best friend is, and I want that. I want someone to come home to most nights. I want someone I can call when I've had a bad shift or someone to celebrate with when things are great.

I suck in a deep breath, holding it for a few seconds before I let it out in a whoosh. I look out the window again and see Lee getting out of his truck. He is that quintessential southern boy. He has all the swagger in his jeans, boots, and a tight T-shirt pulling across his biceps.

I open the front door before he can reach it, leaning against the jamb as I watch him close the distance from my driveway to the porch.

"Hey," I greet, holding my hand up in an awkward-as-fuck wave. I mentally smack myself in the forehead for being so nervous and stupid.

"Hey, yourself," he greets, stopping just inches in front of me. All that separates us is the threshold of my front door. "Can I come inside, or are we talking out here?" he asks, motioning to the two chairs on my porch.

"Sorry," I say, stepping aside and letting him in.

My front door leads right into the living room, so I head for the chair I have, leaving the couch open for Lee to take a seat on.

"Everything okay?" he asks after taking a seat.

I wring my hands, realizing that I probably look like a lunatic right about now.

"I can't do this," I spit out, almost tripping over my own words.

I can tell I've caught him by complete surprise when his eyebrows just about disappear into his hairline.

"Do this...what?" he asks for clarification.

"This...us," I try and clarify, pointing between the two of us. "I thought I'd be okay with the casual, friends with benefits thing, but I've realized that I'm not. I want more. I want the commitment. I want a real relationship. I want to know you're not out fucking some random woman you meet at the bar."

"I can't offer you more, Allison. That's just not who I am," he states matter-of-factly. He's so strong in his conviction, almost as if he's had to give this speech a time or two before.

"I disagree. You're an amazing man, Lee. You don't give yourself enough credit. Even though we've known each other most of our lives, I'd like to think that I've gotten to know you even better these last few months, and I think you're a great guy. You have so much love to give and a hell of a lot to receive; you just have to let it happen."

"That's just not me," he states again as he stands

from where he sits across from me. "I'm sorry, Allison. I'm going to go before I say or do something to hurt you more. I'm sorry what I could offer wasn't enough. I hope you find what you're looking for," he says before heading out the door. He pauses long enough to pull the door shut behind him. Our eyes lock for a second as he looks over his shoulder just before it latches closed.

I don't hold back my tears as I sink against the chair. I let it all out, crying until I didn't think I could cry another drop. I finally force myself up, stopping in my kitchen to pour a glass of wine, the middle of the afternoon be damned. One glass will not cut it tonight, so I bring the entire bottle with me as I head for my bathroom and turn on the hot water to fill up my jacuzzi tub. I light a couple of candles, placing them around my bathroom to give a soft glow of light. I set my wine glass down on the bath tray before I toss in a bath bomb and then go snag my Kindle from my nightstand before I strip and slip into the hot water.

I sink into the water up to my chin, allowing the heat to relax my tense muscles. My head lulls back on the bath pillow—another gift from Lindsay—and I enjoy the swirling water as the jets keep things moving and hot.

I reach for my glass of wine, gulping down half of it before returning it to the tray. My cell buzzes against the wood of the tray, and I almost want to ignore it. I don't think I can stomach talking to Lee right now. I don't really care what he has to say to me; my heart is battered. Just in case it is someone or something important, I flip my phone over and see a text from Lindsay.

LINDS

Hey! How are you holding up? Lee showed up here a little bit ago, and Tucker's been outside with him since. Didn't appear to be in a good mood.

I'm not. I've cried myself out of tears and am currently soaking away my misery both in the bath and with a bottle of wine.

Oh, babe. Want me to come over? We can have a sleepover. Watch trashy movies and eat our weight in take out and candy. I can even stop and get some ice cream or canned cinnamon rolls. I know they're your favorite.

I don't want to ruin your night. I'll be fine.

We didn't have anything important
going on, just an evening at home.
And even if we did have plans, you
know I'd drop anything at any time
to come to your aide. You're my
ride-or-die, sister from another
mister. You're stuck with me for life,
woman.

Lindsay really is the best friend anyone could have. I smile at her text. They don't come any better than she is. You'll never find anyone more loyal, trustworthy, loving, basically the perfect person ever.

I mean, I won't lock you out if you
showed up, but I'd also feel guilty
asking you to come.

Give me an hour, and I'll be there.
What flavor of ice cream do you
want tonight, and what kind of
candy?

Allison: Anything sweet and salty.
You're the best.

I know you'd do the same for me in
a heartbeat. Now, let me go break it
to Tucker that I'm leaving for the
night. I'll put together an overnight
bag and then stop at the store
before heading over. You enjoy that
bath and wine. That reminds me,
how's the wine supply?

I've got one unopened bottle in the fridge.

<adds wine to list> I've got it covered! See you soon.

I turn on some music before I set my phone back down, then get comfortable once again with my head on the pillow and my eyes shut. I sit this way for a long time, well past the pruned stage of relaxing in the water. Not wanting to still be in the bath when Lindsay arrives, I finally pull the plug on the water and push out of the tub. Once enough has drained out, I flip the shower on and rinse off before I get out and towel dry my now relaxed body. I slip on some lounge pants and a baggy sweatshirt. If we are having an old-fashioned sleepover with junk food and movies, I might as well be in my comfortable clothes.

"I've come bearing gifts!" Lindsay says as she pushes through my front door, each of her hands loaded down with at least two bags, with her overnight bag slung over a shoulder.

"Did you buy out the entire store?" I ask.

"Just the break-up slash heartbreak recovery items. Chocolate, ice cream, wine, and some grocery store Chinese."

"Sounds like the perfect kit," I say, taking two of the bags from her hands. I help unpack the items, putting what needs to be in the freezer or fridge away. I grab two plates, setting them on the counter so we can each make one from the take-out containers. "So, how much does Tucker hate me?" I ask, dumping some Mongolian Beef on my plate.

"He doesn't hate you one bit," Lindsay says as she dishes up some lo mein on her own plate. "He was actually giving Lee a piece of his mind when I stuck my head out at one point. I think he's on your side of all this," she says, pointing at me with her fork.

"Really?" I ask, a little shocked at that news.

"Yep. They've been best friends their entire lives like we have, and Tucker has mentioned he wishes Lee would settle down a few times. Tucker did say that he thought things were changing in Lee's mind since the two of you have been spending so much time together lately. He said he's never really done that with anyone else, so he thought Lee had turned a new leaf, so to speak. Maybe your little talk will be the wake-up call that he needs."

"I don't know, Linds. He was just so stonewalled. Said he couldn't give me any more and got up and walked out. I thought for a split second that he might turn around when our eyes met as he was reaching back to shut the door, but he didn't. He just continued on. Left without another look back."

"I'm sorry, Allison. He's a dummy. Want me to punch him in the balls the next time I see him?" she asks, humor lacing her question.

"As nice as that sounds, no. I wish him no ill will. I just wish he'd realize how much potential we could have together. Everything was just so easy and care-free between the two of us. Hell, the last time we were together, he begged me to stay the night just so he could hold me. You don't just cuddle with a fuck buddy all night."

"I'm sure he's just scared. He's never had a serious relationship, and that's a lot of avoiding commitment being engrained into his brain for the last ten-plus years."

"I guess you're right with that assessment. I hadn't looked at things like that," I tell her as I take one last bite of my food. I'm already so stuffed, and we've only touched the Chinese food. I don't know how we used to eat so much crap when we were kids and having sleepovers like this every week."

"Ready for our first chick-flick?" Lindsay asks once we've finished up our dinner round. I place our dishes in the dishwasher before we take our glasses of wine to the living room. I pull out a couple blankets and extra pillows, and we both get comfortable on the couch before I turn on Netflix and we find a movie to take us away.

I look over, halfway through the movie, catching Lindsay texting on her phone. The slight smile on her lips is like a double-edged sword. One edge I'm extremely happy for her. She's found an amazing man in Tucker, but on the other, I'm a tad bit jealous of what she's found. I want that. I want to have a permanent smile etched on my face because I know I've got someone waiting for me at home. "Tell him you're mine tonight. He'll get you back tomorrow. Don't make me pull out the custody agreement," I say jokingly. Tucker and I have a running joke that we've got split custody of Lindsay now that they're together. With their conflicting work schedules, they have to take advantage of the days and nights they are off at the same time. It was why I was so hesitant to ask her to come over tonight. I didn't want to take one of their nights off together from them.

"He's fine. He pulled out the Jack Daniels and is working on getting Lee drunk. So, it sounds like they're having their own version of a pity party," she says, smirking as she puts her phone back down. We both get pulled back into the movie, our attention not breaking until the credits start rolling up the screen.

"Another movie or something else?"

"I'm good with whatever. This is your pity party, so you tell me what you want to do," Lindsay tells me.

"Feel up to a game?" I ask, not really wanting to watch another movie.

"Sure, Rummy?" she asks.

"Yeah, I haven't played in months," I say, standing to go find a deck of cards. We move to the table, pulling out some snacks to munch while we play cards and BS the time away.

MORNING COMES, AND I JUST ROLL BACK OVER. I DON'T have anywhere to be today, so I attempt to fall back to sleep, but it fails me. I pull my Kindle out and get lost in the story I'm currently in the middle of for the next hour or so until Lindsay wakes up. Like all our childhood years, we crashed together in my bed. She's the sister I never had.

"How are you feeling this morning?" she asks sleepily.

"Eh, I'll be fine. I don't feel like bawling right now, so I take that as a plus."

"Has he tried to contact you since leaving here yesterday?" Lindsay asks.

"Nope, not that I would have responded if he did. I almost ignored your text yesterday, thinking it might have been him."

"I wouldn't have let you ignore me," she says, stretching her hands up high above her head. Her phone starts going off on the nightstand on her side of the bed.

"You're being summoned," I say as I chuckle. I swear Tucker can't go a few hours without Lindsay next to him. He's fallen, and fallen fast for my best friend.

15

LEE

Fᴜᴄᴋ...

I groan as the light from the windows shines brightly in my eyes. I'm definitely not in my room or bed. The lack of black-out curtains and the sun streaming in is the first indication of that. Tucker did his best friend duty and got me drunk last night. Drinking my problems away doesn't usually work, and if the pounding headache I'm waking up with is any indication, it didn't solve my issues last night, either, and has just created more.

My mouth is cotton dry; I'm in desperate need of some water and something for my pounding head. Top that off with something greasy to fill my stomach to soak up any of the leftover alcohol, and I might start feeling human again. I roll from the bed, my feet hitting the carpeted floor in Tucker's guest room. I look for my phone and find it plugged in on the nightstand, and next to it is a bottle of water and four ibuprofen. I'm not afraid to admit that I love him. He's a damn good man and the best friend I could ever ask for. Has never cast judgment on my life's choices, even the stupid ones that have gotten me in trouble over the years. I toss back the pills before emptying the bottle of water.

With a little bit of hydration in my body, I make it entirely out of bed and into the bathroom. A quick shower, and I'm already starting to feel slightly better. Now for some more water, maybe some coffee to help wake me up and food, and I'll be like a new man.

I make my way out to the kitchen, my stomach and nose leading the way as if I didn't know the layout of this house as well as I know that of my own. I find Tucker and Lindsay in the kitchen, she's standing next to the stove, and Tucker's got her pinned between him and the countertop. "Morning," I call out so they know I've joined them.

"Morning," Lindsay calls, looking over Tucker's shoulder at me. "How's the hangover?" she asks, turning to flip something that is in the pan.

"Ugh," I grunt, not yet ready to make sentences or use words.

"That good, huh?" She smirks. "That'll teach you to let this man get you drunk. Did you drink anything besides shots of JD?" she asks.

"I don't think so," I tell her honestly, not really remembering much after the first half-dozen or so shots.

"Nope, I kept it to just the Jack Daniels. Didn't need him puking all over the place because of some mixed liquors," Tucker states.

Lindsay slides some eggs onto a plate, along with a few strips of bacon and sausage links, topping the plate off with a few slices of buttered toast, and then sets it all down in front of me.

"You are a godsend," I tell her, picking up the fork and shoveling the hot food into my mouth.

"Hey, that was supposed to be my plate," Tucker whines.

"Hush now, I'll make you another one. Lee looked like he needed it more than you did," Lindsay says to him before kissing him on the cheek.

"You didn't poison this, did you?" I ask, stopping once the food is half gone.

"Nope, but I do have some strong words for you,

but I'll let you recuperate a little bit before I let you have it," she states.

"Shit, son. You're in deep shit, and I am here for it," Tucker quips, fighting back his laughter.

"Hey now, I thought you were supposed to be my best friend."

"I am, but it doesn't mean I can't sit back and laugh at your expense when you're getting your ass handed to you by my woman," he states, sitting on a stool next to me. Lindsay sets down a second plate, filled just as full as mine, with all the same delicious-looking food.

She holds up a coffee pot and an empty cup, offering it to me. "Want a cup?"

"Yes, please." She sets it down in front of me, filling it up to the very brim. I sip down a little bit of the hot liquid, feeling the caffeine hit my bloodstream almost instantly. I might have drunk an unknown amount of whiskey last night and woken up hungover as fuck, but I'm doing pretty good right about now.

"Okay, give it to me," I instruct Lindsay once we've all finished our breakfast and the kitchen has been cleaned up, the dishes loaded into the dishwasher. I'm kicked back in Tucker's recliner while the two of them are curled up together on the couch. I swear he has to be touching her at all times when they're in the same room.

"I'll keep this as short and sweet as I can and get it all out. Then I won't rehash things with you unless you specifically ask me to," she says, pausing to take a deep breath. "I understand you're an adult and can make your own decisions, but I think you royally fucked up yesterday. Allison is one of the best people that you will ever meet, as you well know. She's kind and loyal to a fault. I know it's your 'thing'." she says, using air quotes as she says that last word, "being a lifelong bachelor, but do you really think that will keep you happy for the rest of your life? Think of how much your parents enjoy having you and your siblings over for family events, and how excited your mom was when your sister got engaged, and now to have grandkids on the way. Thinking you can't do all of that and be happy simultaneously is just garbage. You're a good man, Lee. You deserve to find someone who loves you, all of you. All your quirks, all the good and the bad. We all deserve that. Since we were babies, Allison has been my best friend, and I want what's best for her, so if that truly isn't you, then so be it. But don't run just because that is what you've always done. If you think you could make something of it with her, then give it a shot. I know she might be mad for me telling you this, but I haven't seen her as happy as I did for the few months that the two of you were hooking up. She had lost that spark that makes Allison... well, Allison. You brought that back, and I hate that she might lose it again."

I digest everything that Lindsay just word vomited all over me. I've known for a while Allison was special. Hell, I've probably known since I crushed on her back in middle school, but I never wanted to ruin the friendship we had.

"Isn't it better for me to break things off now than to wait months or years down the road when I really break hearts?" I ask, my mind racing with what-ifs.

"Why focus on things ending? What if you give things a go, and you get fifty or sixty happy years together?"

I just shrug my shoulders in reply. She's got me on that question. If I'm being totally honest with myself, I *can* see myself settling down with Allison. Doing the whole marriage and kids thing. But, that part of my brain that loves the bachelor life's freedom throws all the what-if scenarios my way.

"I'm not saying that you need to show up at her

house with a ring in your pocket and profess your undying love to her, but showing up with a bouquet of flowers, a pint of mint chocolate chip ice cream with an apology, and a promise to give things a try, might get you back in her good graces," Lindsay tells me.

"Okay," I tell her, still digesting everything. "I've got some soul searching to do," I say honestly.

"I'd agree with that statement," Lindsay says.

"I think I'm going to head home, do some thinking. Thanks for taking care of me last night," I tell Tucker as I stand from the recliner. I grab the few things that are mine and head for my truck, leaving the two of them on the couch to do whatever happy, in-love people do when left alone.

***

I MAKE IT HOME, HEADING STRAIGHT FOR MY bathroom to take another quick shower, this time putting on clean clothes now that I'm home. I slip into some sweats and an old, faded T-shirt from my early years at the firehouse. Once dressed, I kick back on my bed and scroll through my Facebook feed. I stopped to look at some pictures my sister posted last night of her and my brother-in-law.

They're on a "babymoon" vacation in California. Seeing my sister so happy puts a smile on my face. Anyone can see how much she loves her husband, just as one can see how much he loves her back. The jealousy hits me out of left field. The reality that I *do* want that in my life and not the loneliness I often have when I'm home comes over me.

As much as my house is my sanctuary and a place to just get away from everyone and everything and unplug, it can also be tranquil and lonely.

I pull up Allison's profile, clicking on the last album she's uploaded to. I flip through all the images she's posted in the last few weeks, stopping at one that is of the two of us. It's from not long ago. The night we sat outside Tucker's place, around the bonfire, talking and laughing for hours. Lindsay or someone else at the party must have snapped it of us, as we're not looking at the camera, and I don't remember it being taken. The way we're looking at each other reminds me of my sister's pictures. The mutual attraction and chemistry between the two of us almost jumps off the screen. I royally fucked things up; I only hope I can fix it.

16

LEE

Three weeks later

I'M NOT USUALLY ONE FOR ELABORATE, THOUGHT-OUT plans, but I mulled over how I would redeem myself all day. I know I fucked up, so here's my Hail Mary pass to see if I can recover the biggest fumble of my life.

I take Lindsay's suggestions to heart, stopping at the florist and grocery store. I buy the largest bouquet they have available before grabbing a container of ice cream, some toppings to go with it, and a wine bottle for good measure.

I didn't want Allison to tell me not to bother coming over, so I conveniently never texted or called her to ask if I could stop by. I figured grand gestures are supposed to be a surprise, so here I am, pulling into her driveway about to put it all on the line.

I grab my purchases before hopping out of my truck. As I climb the two steps onto her porch, the door opens as Allison fills the doorway.

"Lee," she greets me, the hesitation lacing her voice noticeable.

"These are for you," I say, handing over the flowers. "I also brought some ice cream and wine," I say a bit awkwardly as I hold up the plastic bags from the grocery store.

"Thanks, you didn't have to bring me anything," she says, blowing out a breath. She sets the flowers down on a table just inside her door, then takes the bags from me. "Did you come over just to bring me these things, or did you need something?" *There's my sassy woman.*

"I-I came to apologize. I know I fucked up a few weeks ago, I said things I regret. I was letting my past dictate my future. In a messed up, roundabout way, I was attempting to protect my heart, only to realize in the process, I was simultaneously breaking yours." I pause to take a break and to let my words sink in as I wait for any kind of reaction from Allison.

The smallest of smiles tugs at one corner of her lips, and that is all I need to know that things are going to be okay. I don't care how much of a front she puts on or how much she makes me work for it; I know I'm going to win her back.

"I'm sorry, can you repeat that?" she asks.

"What part, exactly?" I ask, allowing my cockiness to come out just a little bit.

"The part that you admit to fucking up, being wrong. Wait, let me get my phone so I can record you saying it." She cracks an even larger smile, and I know she's fucking with me now.

I crowd into her space. Cupping her cheek with one of my hands and tilting her face up to mine. "Please tell me I've still got a chance. That you'll forgive me for before. I'm here to beg if I have to. I want you, and *only* you. For as long as you'll have me."

"You're sure about that? What if I want you forever?"

"Then forever better take its time coming," I tell her before crashing my lips to hers.

I pick her up, my hands cradling her ass. God, it feels good to have her back in my arms. I know I fucked up, but that's in the past. She's here in my arms. I'll grovel every day for the rest of my life if I have to, in order to make it up to her.

Pinning Allison to the wall, I remove my hands

from her ass and rip open the buttons on her blouse. The buttons go flying; I'm not being careful, and I don't care. It feels like it's been way too long since I've had this woman beneath me. Her sweet pussy squeezing around my cock. "God damn, you're so fucking beautiful," I tell her, taking in the swell of her breasts. Thank the Lord in heaven for whoever invented the front-closure bra. I snap it open with one flick and find her already hardened nipples.

"Lee," she moans my name as I greedily suck one into my mouth. I sink my teeth onto it, biting to leave a mark—my mark—on her skin. She's mine. I'm hers—forever, by the sounds of it.

"I hope you don't have any special connection to this thong," I growl against her skin as my hand makes it up and under her skirt. I wrap my fingers around the fabric and rip it clear off her body.

"Nope," she gasps. I bring my mouth to hers, greedily sucking at her tongue as I fumble with my jeans. I finally free the button and lower my zipper far enough to push them and my boxers down my hips enough to release my cock. I align my tip with her entrance. I break our kiss, pulling back far enough to look Allison in the eyes.

"Tell me if I need to stop and relocate us to get a

condom." I can't believe I was almost going to sink inside her without wrapping shit up.

"I'm on birth control and clean," she says.

"I'm clean, and I've never not used one," I tell her honestly.

"I trust you, Lee," she says, and my heart skips a beat at her words. "Now, fuck me."

"I don't have to be told twice," I growl before taking her lips with my own once again. I line my cock up with her entrance and plunge in until I'm balls deep. The feeling of being inside her with nothing separating the two of us has my balls pulling up tight and ready to blow. I start running stats through my mind, thinking of the worst calls I've responded to, anything I can think of to keep my orgasm from ending things too early.

"Harder," Allison moans. I do my best to shift her against the wall. I slip my arms under her legs, my hands going to her ass to help raise and lower her on my cock.

The room is filling with the sloppy sounds of our bodies connecting. Our mutual moans and cries of pleasure as we both make our way towards that cusp and then topple over the edge of no return. I hold her ass in my palms, slamming my cock in as deep as I can get it as my orgasm barrels out of me. My knees go weak as stars start spinning behind my eyelids. I stumble around, finding the couch to fall back onto, keeping Allison in my lap, my cock still buried inside her tightness.

"Now that was some make-up sex." She chuckles as we both catch our breath.

"That was just the beginning." I wink at her, pushing her messed up hair from her face.

"I'm okay with that." She smiles at me. A real smile. One that fills her face. Lights up her eyes.

I might have once been okay with just a night, just a quick fuck, just a kiss... but she's taught me that what I really wanted was so much more.

EPILOGUE
LEE

18 months later

I CHECK MY PHONE FOR WHAT FEELS LIKE THE millionth time today. I've done it so many times, I'm sure Allison must think that I'm cheating on her or something shady is going down. Unbeknownst to her, the complete opposite is happening. I'm waiting on Reese Blackwood, a local celebrity and my girl's best friend's cousin, to get back to me if she can help me with my proposal later this weekend. Reese is in town for a large country festival that is taking place this weekend, along with a shit ton of other performers.

"Can you put that thing down?" Allison asks, scrunching her nose at me.

"Sorry, sweetheart. Just waiting on a text," I assure her. "When is Lindsay going to be here?" I ask, trying to get her focus off of me and my phone.

"She texted about ten minutes ago that they were just leaving to pick Paisley up and then would be headed this way."

"So they should be here soon, then, I'd guess."

"Yep, and I can't wait to see how excited Paisley is when she gets to the concert."

"I can't believe she's finally old enough to go to a concert," I muse. My best friend has been a single dad for six years now and has done a hell of a job co-parenting with Paisley's mom. She was a surprise to both of them, but they turned that surprise into the best gift two people could get.

"Uncle Lee, Uncle Lee!" the little angel calls out as soon as the front door opens.

"There's the princess!" I hold my arms out for her to run and jump into.

"Look at my new boots Daddy and Lindsay got me," she says, pointing to the pink cowgirl boots she's got on.

"Wow! Those are pretty cool! Lots of sparkles."

"They were my favorite ones," she tells me as she wiggles to be let down.

"I can only imagine why." I chuckle at her excitement. "Are you excited for today?" I ask her just as I feel my phone vibrate in my pocket.

"Yes! I get to see Reese sing! Do you think she'll let me sing with her?" she asks me.

"Maybe if you ask really, really, *really* nicely."

"Okay." She accepts my answer.

Lindsay has Allison occupied, so I slip my phone from my pocket, checking the screen for my notifications.

REESE

Everything is a go! When you guys arrive, just come to the backstage gate, and you're all on the list to get through. I'll introduce you to my tour manager, who will take care of the rest. Hillary and the guys are really excited to be in on everything, as well.

LEE

Thank you so much! We should be headed that way shortly.

I slide my phone in my pocket, a little weight lifted off my shoulders, knowing that my plan is in the works. By the end of tonight, I'll hopefully have a fiancée and not just a girlfriend.

"You ready, man?" Tucker asks, the girls still occupied.

"As ready as I'll ever be. You've got the ring box, right?" I question him.

"It's safe with me," he says, tapping his pocket. Allison would never suspect a box to be in Tucker's pocket, but in mine, it would stick out like a sore thumb.

"Reese just texted that she's got me covered for tonight," I tell him. Lindsay was the one that suggested this idea to me a month or so out when I started talking to her about helping me plan something, as well as picking out the ring. I would never have thought to reach out to her cousin to see if I could propose on stage at a country concert, but she was all for it. Thought that Allison would love it. "Lady A is willing to help out, as well."

"That's awesome, man. I'm happy for you. You couldn't have picked a better woman."

"Thanks, man. I don't think I would have won her back if it wasn't for your wife, so I've got her and you to thank for making me pull my head out of my ass and see everything that was good right in front of me."

"Are you two ready to go, or are you going to sit around gabbing like we do?" Lindsay asks, smiling over at us.

"We're just waiting on you, ladies," Tucker

drawls at his wife. She walks over to where he's standing and pulls him into a kiss. They keep it somewhat pg13, seeing as his daughter is in the room.

"Okay, love birds, let's get out of here," Allison says, coming to stand at my side. I slide my hand into hers, linking our fingers and squeezing them quickly three times in what's become our thing. A quick three squeezes are our way of telling one another *I love you.* It took me a little while to realize that is what I was feeling for Allison, and even longer to admit that I didn't need to be afraid of that feeling. When I finally embraced it, life got a whole lot better for me.

We pile into Tucker's truck, mainly because it has Paisley's booster seat installed in it. The drive over to the fairgrounds isn't far, just on the outskirts of town.

"Do you know if Jackson and Holly are coming out today?" Allison asks.

"I believe so; Jackson was talking about it before we got off shift yesterday. He said Holly was pretty excited about it."

"Oh, yay! I haven't seen her in a while. I'm excited we'll get to hang out together," Allison says.

Jackson is one of the newest guys on our shift. He moved back to town when a spot opened up in the department and met Holly on his first day on shift when he joined Tucker and me at Holly's school for a program we did for her class. They were pretty smitten from that first meeting.

"When do we get to see Reese?" Paisley pipes up.

"We can go see her as soon as we get there," Lindsay tells her. "She texted me that she was ready for her Paisley girl."

"Mommy, do you think she'll let me help her sing?" Paisley asks Lindsay. It sometimes catches me off guard when Paisley calls Lindsay mom, but she started doing that on her own after Tucker and her married.

We finally pull into the parking lot, finding a spot about halfway back. Not bad for how many people will eventually be at this festival. They have some areas dedicated to people with RV's and campers who stay out here all weekend long, and other areas for those of us that drive in or just come for some of the events.

Once Paisley is out of the truck, she slips her hands into one of Tucker's and mine. We've walked with her like this more times than I can count in her life. She loves to swing between us as we walk across the dirt lot.

We make our way to the backstage gate, and sure enough, our names are all on the list. We're handed badges that will allow us to come and go as we please while here today.

"Hey, guys!" Reese greets as she opens the door to her tour bus and lets us in. It's a little tight with all of us, plus her husband Austin and her daughter, but we make it work.

"Reese!" Paisley calls out as she launches herself at Reese, wrapping her arms around her body.

"Paisley, girl! You've gotten so big!" she tells her as she picks her up.

"I'm six now," Paisley tells her, holding up her fingers. She finally asks her burning question that she's asked all of us multiple times in the past few weeks. "Can I sing with you?"

"You want to sing with me?" Reese asks her.

"Yes! I've been practicing!" she excitedly tells her.

"Well then, I think we'll have to make that happen if your daddy is okay with it," she says, turning her attention to Tucker for approval.

"We told her that it had to be okay with you and your crew."

"It is absolutely okay with me," she tells him.

"How about you come with me to soundcheck in about twenty minutes. We can get you your own microphone and everything."

The look of shock on Paisley's face is everything. This little girl's day has just been made.

"Y'all can come to soundcheck if you'd like. I'll introduce you to the other bands here, if they're around. I think Lady A will be there, maybe Thompson Square, as well."

"That is so cool!" Allison squeals. "I freaking love Lady A."

"Hillary and the guys are so nice; you'll love them!" Reese tells her. I couldn't have planned this better if I tried. Everything just seems to be falling into place today, and from what I can tell, Allison has no clue I'm about to pop the question.

***

"Before I close out my time with y'all tonight, I've got a very special guest to bring on stage. As y'all know, this is my hometown, and I've got a lot of family around. One exceptional little girl is attending her very first concert and wanted nothing more than to help me sing a song tonight. So please, get on your feet and give my little cousin, Paisley, a round of applause."

We all cheer as loud as we possibly can from our center stage seats. She walks out all proud-like, her sparkly boots flashing with the spotlights hitting them. If she's nervous, you can't tell one bit with the confidence that she struts with. She helps Reese belt out one of her early hits, and the crowd sings along. Lindsay is filming the entire thing, which I'm sure Paisley will want to watch a million times over in the coming weeks.

Reese finishes her set, and the stage crews start their quick tear down and set up for Lady A's set, the last one for tonight.

"Hey, Reese is asking if all of us can come backstage for a bit," Lindsay says, holding up her phone as if to show off the text she just received. Really, this is all just part of the plan.

It's go time!

Allison

Something is going on. What that is, I have no freaking idea, but something is going on. Not only has Lee been acting weird, but so has Lindsay. I've been trying to figure out what it could be, but nothing is adding up today. I don't know if I'm just paranoid or what, but I just have a feeling something is up.

"Did you have fun singing on stage?" I ask Paisley when we get backstage to meet up with Reese.

"Yes! Did I do good?" she asks me.

"The best!" I tell her, bopping her nose. She's just so darn cute. "Maybe you can be a professional singer like Reese when you're bigger."

We visit with Reese while the stage is stripped of her equipment and the new stuff is set up. The members of Lady A all come out, readying themselves for their upcoming set.

"Hey, y'all." Hillary Scott, the lead female singer from Lady A, stops at our group. Reese introduced us to them earlier, but I'm still a little tongue-tied being around some of my favorite singers. "We're going to be filming some special shots tonight for a music video; we need some volunteers and are wondering if any of you would be willing to help us out. We just need two of you, preferably a couple," she says.

"We can do it," Lee pipes in. I turn to look at him in shock.

"You want to be in a music video?" I ask him.

"Sure, why not. Sounds kind of fun," he says, giving me a quick peck on the lips.

"I guess we'll do it," I tell her, still not sure what the hell is going on today.

"Perfect!" she says, clapping her hands excitedly. "Just hang out back here; we're going to do it after our opening set; that way, if we need to do a second take, we can."

"No problem, just tell us where you need us and what you need us to do," Lee tells her.

Before we know it, Lady A is going on stage, knocking their opening set out of the park. While they're on stage, their manager comes over and gives us a few pointers on where to stand and what they need us to do. It all sounds simple enough.

Once their song ends, we're shown onto the stage. "We've got some special guests with us tonight. Please welcome, Lee and his lovely girlfriend, Allison," Hillary says to the crowd.

We both wave to the audience; my nerves are turned up to one thousand with all the lights and eyes on us. "We might have told a little white lie to Allison to get her up here," she's saying, but I don't quite register her words. "I'll turn things over to Lee to fill her in on why they're up here with us tonight."

Hillary hands over a microphone to Lee, and it all starts to make so much sense. Him acting off all day, constantly checking his phone. It was all to set this up. Tears burn my eyes as he looks so lovingly into them.

Three quick squeezes to the one hand he holds help calm me as he brings the microphone to his lips.

"Allison, sweetheart," he says, and I can hear people whistling and cheering in the background. I'm doing my best to focus on what he's saying to me at this moment. "With just one kiss, you changed my life all those years ago. Every day I get to spend with you by my side is the best day of my life. It might have taken me a while to figure that out, but I'm so glad I finally did. I can't imagine my life without you in it. Will you marry me?" he asks as he drops to a knee and opens a ring box that I have no idea where he was hiding.

"Yes," I tell him on a sob. My tears have started to leak down my cheeks, but I don't care. All I care about is kissing this man who finally gave love a chance, finally gave us a chance at our forever.

With one final kiss, we find our way off the stage to the cheering of the crowd and the opening chords of "Just A Kiss" by Lady A.

DID YOU LOVE ALLISON AND LEE? YOU CAN READ ALL about Tucker and Lindsay in Rumor Going 'Round!

KISS ME OR NOT - BONUS SHORT STORY
A LYRICS AND LOVE SHORT STORY

Inspired by the lyrics of Are You Going to Kiss me or Not
by Thompson Square

Chapter 1

Jackson

I step out of my truck, sucking in a lungful of the crisp winter air. There is nothing like the first few days when the colder temperatures actually grace us and not the hot and humid days, we usually get around here.

I reach into the back seat of my truck and grab my bag. I always have a change of clothes and a toiletry bag so I can shower after a long shift filled with calls. I've been a fireman for ten years, but today I'm starting over -or at least with a new department. It is the one I always thought I'd work for growing up, but it's funny how life can throw you for a loop and send you on a path you never saw coming.

I take in the large firehouse in front of me as I walk up the sidewalk. I've been here once before when I came in to meet with the fire chief for my final interview. I adjust the strap slung over my shoulder, then reach out and pull the door open. The immediate smells wafting from the kitchen hit my nose, and I'm instantly hungry. It doesn't take me long to find my way inside and to the kitchen. I take in everyone that is milling around. A couple people are in the kitchen area prepping breakfast for the crew who are all sitting around salivating.

"Hey, can we help you?" Someone calls out. I drop my bag to the floor at my feet before addressing the crowd.

"I'm Jackson Montgomery; today is my first day here," I tell the room at large.

"Welcome," multiple people call out.

"Thanks," I state, holding up a hand in a small wave.

"Nice to have you here with us," one of the guys greets, holding his hand out to shake. "I'm Tucker."

"Nice to meet you man, did you grow up around here?" I ask him, as he looks vaguely familiar.

"Sure did, you?" He answers and asks.

"Yeah, over on the other side of town," I tell him.

"Ah, makes sense. I'm not all that familiar with that side of town." Tucker states. "Do you need to go talk to the Chief?"

"I don't believe so; I took care of all the new hire paperwork already."

"Great, after breakfast, we're heading down to the elementary school. We're talking to one of the classes about fire safety, letting them all hop into the truck, try on gear, things like that." Tucker says.

"Sounds fun; I've always enjoyed working with kids," I tell him.

CHAPTER 2

HOLLY

"One – two – three-," I call out as I clap my hands to get my student's attention. "Eyes on me," I follow it up with.

All sixteen of my first graders quickly quiet down, turning their attention to be trained on me.

"We have five minutes before the fire department will be here for our tour of the trucks. I need for all of you to go put your take-home folders in your backpacks and then meet me on the reading carpet on your assigned spot." I give the easy instructions, watching as they all quietly do as instructed.

Just as we're all seated on the carpet, the office ladies buzz in on the intercom. "Ms. Knight, your visitors are on their way down."

"Thank you," I call out.

"Okay, class, let's be on our best behavior for our guests," I remind them, getting sixteen heads nodding up and down, a little excessively in their excitement.

I look up just as a knock against the open door alerts us to the firemen's arrival.

"Hello, come in," I tell them.

"Thank you for having us," one of the guys says. "I'm

Tucker, and this is Jackson and Lee." He introduces everyone.

"Nice to meet you all, I'm Holly Knight, and this is my first-grade class," I tell them, pointing to all the kids. "I figured we could start with the Q&A session before we move outside? Does that work for you guys?" I ask.

"That's perfect. Since everyone is already seated, we can just head over there." Tucker says. I step out of the way, giving them full access to the classroom. I recognize Tucker and Lee, but I don't think I've ever seen Jackson around town before. I can't help but take in the way he fills out a t-shirt that boasts the fire stations' info.

"Hey, everyone!" Tucker greets the kids and gets right into his fire safety presentation. The kids quickly raise their hands to ask questions, and the three guys take turns answering them for everyone. I'm super impressed at how they all keep their answers at a first-grade level.

"You helped my mommy and me when we were in an accident," little Sebastian says when they call on him.

"We help a lot of people, whether it is a fire or a car accident. Were either of you hurt?" Lee asks him.

"No, you let us go home," Sebastian tells him.

"Well, that's good!" Lee tells him.

"What do you all say we go and check out the truck?" Tucker asks, much to my class's excitement.

"Let's line up and remember to use our hall voices on our way outside."

I lead the kids out to the front of the school, where they have the fire truck parked along the front sidewalk. I'm surprised how well they all stay in line and wait for the guys to get things opened and ready for them to check out.

"The gear you see Jackson putting on is called turnout gear. It keeps us safe when we enter burning buildings to save people or to work on putting out a fire. If you are ever in a building that catches on fire, it is best to try and get outside as quickly as possible. If you were to get scared or stuck, you might have a fireman or woman come to find you. It can be scary sometimes when you see one of us approach you, but just know that we're there to help you, and this gear is there to protect us." Tucker explains to the kids.

"Would anyone like to try on our gear?" Jackson asks as he starts to take things off again. I try to hide my ogling of him as he strips back down to his pants and t-shirt.

"Me, me, me!" All of my students call out at the same time.

"How about we take turns. We can split you up into a few smaller groups. One can check out the front part of the truck, one can try on gear, and one can check out the back part of the truck, then we can switch. How does that sound?" Tucker suggests.

"Sounds perfect!" I state, clapping my hands to get my class's attention. I quickly split them up, sending each group on their own way.

Before I know it, our time has come to an end. The kids

had an absolute blast, and I know I'll keep this activity on my to-do list for future classes.

CHAPTER 3
JACKSON

I lean back in the recliner, getting comfortable before the movie starts. We went out on one call after leaving the school this afternoon, but otherwise, it has been a quiet night so far.

An alarm sounds, letting us know someone is at the door. Being the new guy, I stay put and let Lee go and answer it.

"I'm sure the guys will love this; thank you for bringing it over." I can hear him saying as his voice gets closer. The moment he walks around the corner with Holly by his side, I can't stop the reaction my body has to seeing her. My dick twitches to life, especially due to the way her ass fills out the jeans that were made for her. I swear they were cut to only fit her curves.

"Listen up," Lee calls out. "Ms. Knight stopped in to bring us dessert as a thank you for spending time with her class today.

"Thank you, we love it when someone brings dessert." One of the other guys calls out.

"My pleasure. My kids loved having you, and we learned so much. I hope y'all don't mind if I keep the activity on my yearly to-do list. I think it was a great way to make the kids feel more comfortable if they were ever to be in the situation that needed your help."

"We're always happy to help," Tucker tells her. "And you're right; the more we can interact with kids in a normal environment, the less likely they are to be scared of us in an emergency."

I hop up from my recliner, heading to where she's standing next to Lee, and offer to take the large box from her hands. I take it to the kitchen, setting it down on the counter before opening the lid and peering inside to find an assortment of cupcakes. My mouth waters at the sight of them. I snag one, setting it aside before the rest of the guys all descend on the box as well.

I don't want to miss my chance to talk with Holly, so I walk around the island to where she's joined us in the kitchen. "Would you like one of the cupcakes?" I offer.

"No, I'm good, thank you." She smiles up at me. The way my balls tighten at the way her smile fills her face is like no response I've ever experienced.

"I'm Jackson," I introduced myself, shaking her hand.

"I remember, but it's nice to meet you again. You were so great with my students. Do you have kids of your own?" She asks.

"None of my own, just a niece and nephew."

"You must spend a lot of time with them then; you were a natural today."

"I try and see them every chance I get," I tell her honestly.

"I bet they love their uncle Jackson time." She says, and I think I hear a hit of flirtation in her voice.

"What about you, any kids of your own?"

"Nope." She says, popping the p. "I'd like to find a husband first." She tells me, and I don't miss the way her cheeks turn pink with a blush of embarrassment.

"That might be helpful." I chuckle as I answer. "Not to change the subject completely, but what would you say to dinner with me sometime soon?" I ask, taking my shot for a date.

She nibbles on her bottom lip as she looks me over. I can practically feel her eyes on me as they drop down my body and back up, finally stopping once they reach my eyes. The electricity between the two of us is practically combustible.

"I'd love that." She finally says.

"Can I text you my number, and then we can set something up. I work until tomorrow afternoon, then have forty-eight hours off before I have to be back for another twenty-four."

"I'm free tomorrow or whenever. I don't go out much, especially during the week." I reached for my cell while pulling up my contacts app and I added her in. She rattles off her number, and I immediately send a quick text, so she has mine.

"I'm off at three tomorrow; how about I pick you up at four?" I suggest.

"Sounds good," She agrees quickly.

"Do you have a curfew I should be aware of, or can I keep

you out late?" I ask, flashing her a smirk.

"I don't turn into a pumpkin until midnight." She teases.

"I'll keep that under advisement." I wink at her. "I just need your address so I know where to pick you up tomorrow."

"I'll text it to you." She says as she taps away at her phone. Mine buzzes a moment later, and I look at it to see she's sent it to me.

~

I toss my bag into my truck before sliding into the driver's seat. It was a quiet night with no calls, so I'm well-rested for my date with Holly tonight. The holiday festival is happening, and I know there is a concert tonight. I figured that might be an easy way to get to know each other without the pressure of a fancy dinner with the potential of uncomfortable pauses.

I pulled into my driveway of the house I rented just last week when I moved to town to take the job at the firehouse. I take my bag inside the house, then head back out to the garage to fill up the lawnmower to cut the grass. It takes me an hour or so to get it done, including the weed-eating around the edges. I swipe at my sweaty brow with the bottom portion of my t-shirt, giving up and just pulling it off over my head. I stand in my yard, shirtless, as cars drive by, a few of them honking as they go past. I can't help but chuckle at the attention.

Once inside, I grab a large glass of ice water to help cool myself down, and I headed to the shower. I need to clean up before I can do much else. I'm covered in dust and grass clippings as well as sweaty from all the manual labor outside.

~

I pull into Holly's driveway, parking behind her car. I check my reflection in the rearview mirror before cutting the engine and making my way out of the driver's seat. I reach in for the small bouquet of wildflowers I picked up on my way.

I walk down the short walkway, up the two steps onto the porch. Before I can knock or ring the bell, the front door flies open, and the view of Holly about knocks the breath from my lungs. She's standing in front of me in dark jeans, which are tucked into some boots that almost hit her knees, a fitted t-shirt that is mostly covered by a half-buttoned flannel shirt. Her hair is partially pulled back, the strands that were in her face when we met at her school are pinned to the top of her head.

"Hi," she greets, giving me a little nervous wave.

"Hi, yourself." I stupidly replied. "These are for you, and you look amazing tonight."

"Thanks, and you're sure this is okay for whatever we're doing tonight?" She asks, looking down at her clothes with a worried look on her beautiful face.

"You're perfect," I tell her, hoping she gets the deeper meaning of that answer.

"Thank you for these; let me go put them in some water

and then we can get out of here."

"Sounds like a plan," I say, following her inside as I take in the small living room. Her place is very simply decorated. A couch and TV are the two large items in the living room. She's got a few more personal touches than I do, but it is clear she's a simple girl that likes to be comfortable.

"How was your shift?" Holly asks once we are in my truck and rolling down the road.

"Pretty quiet, actually," I tell her.

"Is that a good thing?" She asks.

"It's a double-edged sword. On the one hand, it is nice to actually get some sleep when you're on for so long at one time, but on the other, if you don't get any calls, then the hours practically crawl by."

"That makes sense. Do you often have shifts with no calls?"

"I can't speak yet for this house, but at my last firehouse, it wasn't a common thing. We'd usually get a few calls each shift."

"How long have you been a firefighter?" She asks.

"I went into the academy at twenty-one, so eleven years ago."

"Wow, did you follow anyone's footsteps?"

"Nope. But after a field trip to a firehouse when I was in the third grade, I was enamored with fire trucks. After high school, I worked and saved until I finally got accepted into the academy. Once in, I put my head down and focused on being the best that I could be."

"That's some dedication. What made you move?"

"It's been worth all the hard work. My parents are here, and they're getting older. I wanted to be near them so that if they need me for anything, I'm not hours away. Now I'm just across town and can check in on them and be here if they need me."

"I love that family is so important to you," she says, and I can't help but like that fact.

"Of course, I know firsthand how quickly something can happen, and you can lose those that are important to you. I want to make the most of my time with them."

"I couldn't agree more."

"Did you always want to become a teacher?" I ask, as I pull into the parking lot and find a spot.

"I did. I've always enjoyed kids, and teaching seemed like the logical answer. I was a nerd and loved school, so it's fitting that I now work in one."

"Passionate teachers make a lasting impression. I have fond memories of the teachers who meant the most to me."

"I can only hope I make a lasting impression on my students."

"I'm sure you will."

"It's still so surreal when former students come back to see me. My first class is now in eighth grade. That makes me feel so old." She chuckles.

"You're not old." I deadpan, looking at her and running my eyes up and down her body. I don't miss the way her skin pinks up as she blushes. "Let's go," I say, opening my door and getting out. I round the front of the truck and make it to her door before she opens it.

I hold my hand up, offering it to her as she slips out of my truck. Once her feet are on the ground, she takes my offered hand, slipping her small one into my large one.

"Shall we?" she asks, looking up at me. The light dances in her eyes, and I want nothing more than to kiss this woman.

I clear my throat, suddenly feeling like I've got something stuck in it. "We shall," I state before starting to walk toward the entrance for the holiday festival. The ticket booth has garland and lights wrapped around it, as do the light poles lining the sidewalk. I even noticed the festive mistletoe randomly placed in different spots. I'll have to see if we can just happen to stop beneath a branch at some point tonight.

"Two tickets, please," I tell the teenager in the booth.

"Here's the schedule of events; if you want to go to the concert tonight, the gates for that open at six. It is general admission unless you have the VIP tickets, which are sold out."

"Thanks," we both tell her at the same time.

"What should we check out first?" I ask Holly. She's scanning the schedule as I guide us down the sidewalk and into the fairgrounds where the festival is being held.

"Let's go look at the Christmas trees! I always love seeing how creative everyone is," she says, and I can tell she's excited by the added bounce in her step.

"Lead the way," I tell her. I know we've only known one another for a day, but I can already tell I'd follow this woman anywhere.

CHAPTER 4
HOLLY

"Was Christmas a big deal for your family when you were growing up?" I ask, as Jackson and I walk through the room filled with decorated trees. At the end of the festival these are all auctioned off with the money going to charities.

"Yes, my mom always went all out with the decorating and baking. I swear she started baking as soon as Thanksgiving was over and didn't stop until Christmas Day. She was known for her sweets and would sell them to people."

"Sounds like my childhood, minus the selling of baked goods," I tell him. "I love the holiday season; it really is my most favorite time of year," I tell him.

"What was the best present you ever got growing up?" he asks.

"Oh, wow. That's a hard one." I say, mulling over memories of past gifts. "If I can only pick one, it would probably be the time my dad surprised all of us with a trip. He'd planned everything and somehow kept it completely a secret, even from my mom."

"Brave man. Where did he take you?"

"On a cruise! We left the day after Christmas. It was a bit crazy having to pack on such short notice, but we did it and made some amazing memories on that trip." I tell him, thinking back to that time. "What about you? What was your favorite gift?"

"My parents always did their best to provide, but extras were hard to come by. There were many years that the only thing under the tree were homemade gifts. One year I got a baseball bat, glove, and ball and played with that set for hours. I played with it until the stitching all came out of the ball, and the glove would no longer fit my hand. It was probably the best-used gift they got me."

"I love that even though you weren't getting tons of presents, holidays are still important to you. It goes to show you've got good character. Materialistic things will only get you so far in life, but family and time with them is something you can't ever get back."

"Exactly." He agrees. "I swear you're like no one I've ever met. Most women are all about what I should buy them and how much money I make, or how big a house they think I need. Hearing you say that makes me want to kiss you right now."

I stop walking and turn to face him. I smile up at him once we've made eye contact. I'm not usually so forward, but there's just something about Jackson that makes me feel so comfortable as if I'm with an old friend. "Are you going to kiss me or not?" I brazenly ask.

"Such pressure." He muses. He takes his sweet ass time, cupping my cheek with his big, calloused hand, one that I can tell is strong, and I want to feel all over my body. His thumb slides along my bottom lip, and I can't help but flick the tip of my tongue out, licking it as he passes over it once more. I watch as his eyes dilate a little more. He steps ever-so closer, closing the few inches that separated us, and I swear it happens in slow motion. He dips his head, inching closer until finally, his lips crash against mine. I don't give him a second to think before I'm opening for him. Our tongues collide, dueling it out as he kisses the breath right out of my lungs.

I have no idea how much time passes before we break apart. It could have been ten seconds or ten minutes. All I know is I want more, so much more from this man.

"What are you doing to me, woman?" he asks, pressing his forehead against mine.

"I'd like to ask you the same thing," I tell him.

"Let's keep moving, or I might do something that will get us both arrested." He smirks.

"That probably wouldn't go over very well with either of our bosses." I laugh.

"No, it wouldn't, but there'll be more of that later." He says, dropping a quick kiss on my lips before pulling away.

We finish looking at the decorated trees, then head back outside to find some food. Although my stomach is excited about the food, the rest of my body is ready to go somewhere a little more private to get more of those kisses from him.

CHAPTER 5
JACKSON

That fucking kiss is all that I can think of-well that and how she felt in my hands. I can only imagine how her entire body pressed against mine or under mine would feel. I can't think about that, or I'll be sporting a hard-on so big that they'll be no hiding it.

We find a food truck, order our food, and find a picnic table that is open to sit at.

"When does your Christmas break start?" I ask after we've both taken a few bites of food.

"Next Friday is the last day!" she says, and I can tell she's excited. "Then I'm off for two straight weeks. I cannot wait."

"Do you have any big plans for your break?"

"Does sleeping in everyday count?" she asks.

"Not a morning person?" I ask, quirking a brow.

"Ugh, I'd like to not be one, but on school mornings I have to be up around five-thirty to get everything done and to school on time."

"What do you have to do in the mornings, and what time do you have to be at school?" I ask.

"I go to the gym every morning, then shower, get ready, eat a quick breakfast, and get to school by seven-thirty. That gives me time to prep anything I didn't get done the day before. Some mornings we have short staff meetings or grade-level meetings, and then the kids start arriving at five after eight."

"Sounds like a well-oiled routine. What do you do in the summers?"

"I have a part-time job at the bookstore here in town. I love to read, so the employee discount comes in handy, plus it gives me something to do and a little extra money in my pocket. Teachers don't make a lot, so I have to supplement my income."

"What's your preferred genre to read?" I ask.

"Romance." She boldly tells me, and I can see a flash of determination in her eyes.

"Like bodice ripper-Fabio on the cover romances?" I ask, remembering seeing those types of books around because my mom and grandmother would get them from the library and share them.

"Kind of, I'm not so much a fan of those, but more contemporary romances. Things set in a more modern time. Don't get me wrong, a good historical romance hits the spot every once and awhile, but I'd rather be reading about sexy firemen or hockey players and the women that they sweep off their feet."

"Sexy firefighters, you say?" I ask, raising my eyebrows at her.

"Oh yes, there are some *hot* firefighter books out which

require a firehose to put out the flame they cause, " she says, but can't keep from cracking up at the pun.

"You'll have to share one with me sometime. Maybe I can tell you if they're realistic or not." I wink at her and love the way she blushes.

A commotion pulls our attention toward the stage where the concert is happening tonight. "I wonder what's going on," Holly says, standing to toss her trash away.

"We can go check it out if you'd like" I offer, following behind her.

"Sure, it's probably the band just getting ready for their set."

I grab her hand, linking our fingers together again. I'm quickly loving the feeling of touching her any way I can. We walk toward the stage area, and the commotion is still going on.

"Holy crap! Reese is here!" She says, turning to me with a massive smile on her face.

"Reese?" I ask?

"Yes, Reese Blackwood, I'm sure you've heard of her a time or two. This is her hometown, and she comes back all the time. She must be playing a set tonight."

"Do you want to go find a place to sit?" I offer.

"Yes, but let's go say hi. I haven't seen her in almost a year."

"Do you know her-know her?" I ask.

"Of course, we grew up together. She doesn't spend much

time here now that she's married and has kids. Her husband plays hockey for the Indianapolis Eagles."

"Cool, I didn't know all that," I tell her honestly.

"She's probably the most famous person to come from this area of Georgia," she tells me as we make our way over to the large crowd of people. As we get closer, I can now see that there is, in fact, a woman in the center of the crowd that everyone is trying to talk to. We wait, eventually making it up to her. I just stand back as Holly and Reese squeal and hug in that way that only two girlfriends can do after not seeing one another for a long time.

"Holly! I'm so happy that I got to see you. I would have texted or called to let you know that I was coming, but it was literally a last-minute decision. Austin is out on the road for the week with some away games and I didn't really want to sit around the house when I could come home to see family. How's life?" She asks her.

"It's great. This is Jackson," She introduces us, and I don't miss the way that Reese gives me a once over. "Jackson, this is Reese."

"Nice to meet you, ma'am," I greet her back.

"Oh, he's a keeper." Reese says, "Manners and muscles. Girl, you've done good."

"Oh, stop it. We're actually on our first date." Holly tells her.

"Then don't let me keep you. I'll call or text you before I

leave town. Maybe we can grab lunch or something. I want to hear everything."

"Sounds good," Holly tells her before they hug again, and we move on so the next person can talk to Reese.

We stop at one of the vendors, and I buy a blanket for us to sit on and two hot chocolates to help keep us warm as the sun sets and the cold creeps in.

"So, what was that about muscles and manners?" I tease Holly once we've found a place to sit and wait for the concert to start. "Did I understand that makes me a keeper?"

"Ugh, let's agree to forget that you heard that comment." She says, leaning back against me as we sit on the blanket.

"I kind of liked it; it sounded like a compliment," I tell her as I move her hair from her shoulder, exposing her neck to me. I can't help but brush my lips against the skin, watching as it breaks out in goosebumps. I also don't miss the entire body shiver that it causes.

"You're trouble," she muses, turning so she can look up at me.

"Only with you," I tell her before I eagerly kiss her. I've been waiting for the moment I could do this again. I swear her lips were made for mine. I slowly slide my tongue along hers, wishing that I was sliding my cock inside her at the same rhythm.

I kiss her for a few minutes, forcing myself to keep my hands on her face and neck only. I don't need those pesky indecent exposure arrest charges. "You're trouble," I tell her after breaking the kiss.

"I know you just paid money for this blanket so we could watch the concert, but I'd be okay with skipping it and getting out of here," she says.

I can't get her up fast enough. Once I'm standing and we're off the blanket, she picks it up, folding it over her arm haphazardly. Before we walk away, I pick her up, tossing her over my shoulder in a fireman's carry.

"Jackson!" she squeals and smacks my ass as I beeline it for the parking lot.

CHAPTER 6
HOLLY

"Jackson!" I holler again, smacking his ass multiple times as he practically runs with me over his shoulder.

"Just hold still, woman." He says. There isn't much else I can do, so I hold on tight until he finally puts me down on my own two feet.

"Was that really necessary?" I ask. as the blood rushes back down my body. I can't help but laugh at how quickly he moved.

"Darlin', when a beautiful woman basically tells you to take her home, you don't waste a second doing just that," he says before backing me up against the side of his truck and kissing me hard. I run my hands up his abs, feeling the ridges through his clothes. I find the hem of his shirt and slip my fingers underneath, toying with the waistband of his jeans. I slide to the middle, finding his happy trail to play with. "Fuck woman." He growls against my lips.

"Take me home, Jackson," I tell him.

He quickly opens the door, waiting for me to get in before he closes the door. I watch as he rounds the front, practically jogging to get to the driver's side.

"In a hurry?" I tease, as he peels out of the parking lot.

"Yep, to make you scream my name." He smirks.

"Tell me more." I toss right back at him. This back-and-forth banter is the best foreplay I've ever experienced. Hell, this entire night is something new for me. I've never had sex on the first date, but I want this man like I want my next breath. I can't exactly explain why that is, but I'm going to just go with it. Fate has a funny way of making things work when you least expect it to.

Jackson pulls into his driveway, and I take in the cute little house. It isn't extravagant, but the perfect place for a single guy. He cuts the engine, and I'm a little surprised he doesn't immediately get out. For how quickly he got us out of the fairgrounds, I'd have thought he'd be a little quicker to get us inside his house.

"Something wrong?" I finally ask, breaking the silence.

"No," he shakes his head, looking me dead in the eyes. "I just don't want to rush this, rush you. If this is all too fast, just tell me. Don't get me wrong, I want you-hell I need you like I need my next breath, but if you need to wait, I'll understand and do just that."

I reach over, placing my palm on his cheek. He nuzzles into it, and I love the scratchiness of his stubble against my skin. I can practically feel it between my thighs. The groan that falls from his lips tells me that he didn't miss the way that I rubbed my thighs together, looking for a bit of friction.

"Woman, you're going to kill me," he says before kissing my palm.

"Jackson, I don't want to slow down; I don't want to stop. I want you to take me inside and make me scream your name."

"Yes, ma'am," he says before the urgency returns. We're both out of the truck, and he's carrying me, thankfully this time not over his shoulder, into his house.

He takes me straight to the bedroom. I'm deposited on the bed, then left. I wait for a second, then hear the click of a lamp as it floods the room with light.

I lean back on the bed, watching as he moves back in front of me. He pulls his shirt off over his head, exposing all those muscles I've wanted to get my eyes on since the first time he walked into my classroom. I could only imagine what they looked like then, and boy, oh boy, they don't disappoint, one bit. This man doesn't skip ab day at the gym.

He pops the button on his jeans, then lowers the zipper. "Are you going to join me or is this a one-sided strip show?" he asks, running his fingers up my thigh.

"I was quite enjoying the show," I tell him, reaching out to run a hand along with his abs.

"I can keep going if you'd like," he offers. He pushes his jeans down a little further, exposing the top of his groin area. I sit up a little straighter, waiting for the moment his cock springs free from the confinement of his jeans and boxers.

"Holy shit" I call out, as his cock bobs in front of me. I can't help but wrap a fist around it, stroking him before I bring my lips to the tip and suck it into my mouth.

"Holly!" He shouts my name as his hands sink into my hair. I flick my tongue along his crown, learning what works for him as I blow him.

He drops one hand from my hair, cupping my breasts over my shirt. He pinches at my nipples, causing them to harden, even though they are still fully covered with my clothes. He pulls his cock from my grasp, with the pop of it leaving my mouth filling the room.

"I need you naked," he growls, leaning down to kiss my swollen lips. We both work on removing my clothes, our lips staying locked together.

Once we're both naked, he laid me down on the bed, covering me with his large body. "My turn to worship you," he says, sliding down and kissing his way around my body. The anticipation of where he'll kiss me next has me so on edge that I'm ready to combust.

"You like that?" he says against my skin. He flicks my nipple with his tongue as his thumb flicks in the same rhythm against my clit.

"Yes," I pant, just about ready to lose it and come from nipple and clit stimulation only.

"Come for me, Hol," He instructs, and I do just that as he presses down on my clit and sucks my nipple into his mouth. My body clenches as the tidal wave of pleasure takes over. My body goes rigid before I go limp. I can't even describe the feeling. It is just that blissful.

"So beautiful," I hear him say in my foggy state.

He slides inside me, my body instantly clenching around him. The intrusion of his hard cock has my orgasm doubling down. "Jackson!", I sob his name.

"Yes, Hol, just go with it. Let it all out." He coaches me through my orgasm. Once my body has stopped spasming, he starts to rock his hips. The feeling is better than anything I've experienced before. "You were made for me.," he says before kissing me gently. His easy rocking builds speed and becomes a fast thrust as he works us both up. I can feel him swell inside me before he crests over the edge of his own orgasm, taking me with him as I come again. The way his pelvis hits my clit as my body is so overwhelmed with pleasure, I don't know that I'll ever fully recover from this night.

"I'll be right back." He says a few minutes later. He rolls away from me, and instantly I miss the warmth and security I felt with him by my side. He removes the condom and tosses it in the trash. He comes back a minute later with a wet washcloth in his hand, offering it to me to clean up with. I do so but take it with me back to the bathroom before I meet him back in bed.

"I can practically hear you thinking," Jackson says a while later. We've been lying in bed, snuggled up together as we both just lay here. The hum of the heater is the only sound filling the room. "What are you thinking about?" he asks, tightening his grip on me.

"Umm," I stall; I don't know what to tell him. I've never, *ever,* done something this spontaneous, but I also don't regret it. "I just don't know what comes next. Was this a one-night stand for you? I've never done this, been this spontaneous." I told him.

"I won't lie and tell you I've never had a one-night stand because I have. Once. But, no, I don't want this to be a one-time thing. From the moment I walked into your classroom, I've felt this pull toward you. I can't explain it. I don't know what it means or where this will go, but I'd like to explore it," he tells me, and I can't help but smile.

"I have that same pull toward you. It is unexplainable but also something I'd like to explore. I just don't want you to think I'm some slutty person who sleeps with anyone I go on a date with."

"I wouldn't think that, and even if you had slept with every guy you've gone on dates with, as long as it was consensual, you're an adult and can decide who you share your body with. I do have one request," he says, tipping my head up so we can look at one another.

"What's that?" I ask.

"While we're exploring this, I want us to be exclusive. No dating anyone else. That goes both ways."

"Of course, I wouldn't even dream of going out with

someone else. I'm a one-man kind of woman," I assure him.

"I like hearing that," he says and rolls us until he's hovering over me. Those bulging biceps are popping out with his body weight resting on his forearms. "Think I can pull a few more orgasms out of you tonight?" he asks, a smirk already tugging at his sexy face as he lowers it to my chest and laps at my nipples.

"I don't know, but I'm up for the challenge," I tell him.

CHAPTER 7
JACKSON

Six Weeks Later

I pull into Holly's driveway, fresh off my latest shift. I'm dead ass tired but ready to see my girl. We haven't seen each other in three days, and that's just too damn long if you ask me.

As soon as I reach the bottom step of the porch, the front door flies open, and Holly is jumping into my arms. I might have been dead-ass tired five minutes ago, but with my woman in my arms, I'm suddenly ready to be awake for hours.

"I've missed you," she says between kisses.

"Not as much as I've missed you," I tell her as I carry her inside.

"Are you ready to meet my parents tonight?" she asks, after I've set her down.

I collapse on the couch, the exhaustion hitting me once again. We were out on back-to-back calls last night and I got very little sleep. "Of course, I am; I just need a nap first," I tell her. Things have gone so smoothly these last few weeks. We basically spend every available hour we can together since that first date. We've become inseparable outside of our work hours.

"Why don't you go take a nap? I'll wake you up in a few hours, then we can leave.

"I have a better idea," I say, pulling her down into my lap. "How about you take a nap with me. I'll wake you up with my tongue between your thighs, and then we can head to your parents."

"You're incorrigible," she laughs and smacks my chest. "And a horny, horny man."

"It's all your fault," I try to blame her. "Whenever I'm around you, I just have to have you.”

"Incorrigible, I tell you." She laughs again. "How about I lay down with you, and then I'll get back up once you're asleep so I can finish my laundry and other things I need to get done around here today."

"But orgasms and my tongue on your clit." I point out.

"I never said that couldn't happen so you can come to find me once you're awake, and I can come back to bed with you." She suggests.

"I guess I can work with that," I state.

"It's settled then." She plants a kiss on my lips. "Now bed."

I slid her off my lap and let Holly help pull me up and off the couch. I link my fingers with hers as she leads me down the hall and into her bedroom. We've flip-flopped about who stays at whose house, but the thought has crossed my mind to ask her to move in with me which would make things that much simpler, but I have to remind myself that it's only been six or so weeks since we met.

Once in the bedroom, I see that Holly is already lying down, looking like the goddess she is. I slide in next to her, my body relaxing as soon as it hits the cool sheets. I pull her in close, loving the feel of her body next to mine as sleep claims me for the next few hours.

CHAPTER 8
HOLLY

Six Months Later

I sit around a bonfire pit, the flames licking at my skin as the wood crackles under the heat of the fire. Jackson and I are at Tucker's place for one of his summer BBQ's that he's become known for. People were all over the place today, but we've weeded it down to just a few couples left sitting around the fire. Tucker's daughter is also here, and she's just the cutest thing ever; I hope that when she makes it to first grade she will be in my class.

"I brought you this," Jackson's voice fills my ears as he kisses my cheek and places a Mike's Hard Lemonade in front of me.

"Thank you," I say, accepting the cold bottle.

"I'm ready to head home whenever you are," he says, sitting behind me on the wood bench. I love hearing him say home. As soon as school ended for the summer, I moved into his house. We've spent the last two months making it perfect for the two of us. It's been a bit of a learning curve, but we've adjusted well overall. I've even been wearing him down on the idea of getting a puppy sometime soon.

"Let me finish this, and then we can go," I say, holding up the bottle he just gave me.

"Take your time; we're in no rush." He claims.

"What if I wanted you to be in a rush?" I ask, and I love the way he holds me tighter. I often tease him over how quickly he whisked me out of the fairgrounds on our first date to get me home and into bed.

"Just give me the word, and I'll sling you over my shoulder any day."

"Okay, caveman," I say.

"What are you two love birds laughing about?" Tucker's fiancé, Lindsay, asks?

"Just giving him a hard time," I tell her.

"I'm sure you are!" She calls back, the innuendo clear as day in her reply.

"Don't encourage her," Jackson says.

We end up sitting around for another few hours, shooting the shit with our friends as the fire burns on. The guys might be paid to put fires out, but I've learned that most firefighters actually love starting fires as much as they love putting them out.

~

"Come here, darlin'," Jackson croons once we're finally back home. He's turned on the radio; an older country song is playing in the background as he pulls me into his arms and starts swaying with me to the melody. I relax into his embrace, soaking up each and every moment we get like this. "Did you have fun tonight?" He asks.

"So much fun; you work with a great group of guys."

"That I do. And it's nice they've all got girlfriends you can hang out with when we get together."

"I've known Lindsay forever; we basically grew up together."

"I know, you've told me all about your shenanigans with her and Reese when y'all were younger."

"Some of the best days of my life were spent with those two," I tell him honestly.

"Good memories to have." He says. The song changes, and it just so happens to be Reese's new single. This one is a slow and sexy song. Jackson pulls me in a tad bit closer, and I rest my cheek against his chest as we move around the living room as if it was a dance floor. "I love you, Holly." He says into the crown of my head. I pull back, tears already leaking from my eyes.

"I love you too," I tell him. The words easily fell from my lips. It's been a long time coming, as we exchanged these three important words.

"Thank fuck." He blows out a huge breath before sweeping me off the floor and into his arms.

"Are you going to kiss me or what?" I ask, not so patiently waiting for him to do so.

"Only every day for the rest of my life." He says and proceeds to do just that.

The End!

COMING SOON

To find out what's next from Samantha, please visit her website at samanthalind.com

ALSO BY SAMANTHA LIND

INDIANAPOLIS EAGLES SERIES

Just Say Yes ~ Scoring The Player

Playing For Keeps ~ Protecting Her Heart

Against The Boards ~ The First Intermission

The Hardest Shot ~ The Game Changer

Rookie Move ~ The Final Period

Box Set 1 {Books 1-3} ~ Box Set 2 {Books 4-6}

Box Set 3 {Books 7-10}

INDIANAPOLIS LIGHTNING SERIES

The Perfect Pitch ~ The Curve Ball

The Screw Ball ~ The Change Up

LYRICS & LOVE SERIES

Marry Me ~ Drunk Girl

Rumor Going 'Round ~ Just A Kiss

STANDALONE TITLES

Tempting Tessa

Then You Came Along

When I Found You

Cocky Doc

Sweet valley, Tennessee

Nothing Bundt Love

Nothing Bundt Forever

San Francisco Shockwaves

Ryker ~ Aiden ~ Tristan

Damien ~ Blake

Austin Fusion

Zack

ACKNOWLEDGMENTS

I have so many people to thank that I sometimes don't know where to start. I'll start with my family. Thank you for encouraging me to write all these stories that keep me up at night. Thank you for all the time you give me to hide away and type all the words!

Renee - I seriously couldn't do this without you! It is crazy sometimes how alike we think!

My multiple author group chats - Procrastinating & Butt Stuff, Chat full of Mommies, OG Girls - Thank you for all the laughs, sprints, and words of encouragement.

My readers! You are the real MVPs here! Thank you for reading my books and loving my characters just as much as I do.

This story was a little harder to write, seeing as it started out as a short story. I knew when I wrote that over a year ago that Allison and Lee had so much more to their story, and I'm so thankful that I could come back to them and tell all of it.

xoxo,

Samantha

ABOUT THE AUTHOR

Samantha Lind is a *USA TODAY* Bestselling contemporary romance author. When she's not dreaming up new stories, she can often be found with her family, traveling, reading, watching her boys on the ice or watching her favorite professional team (Go Knights Go!).

Connect with Samantha in the following places:
www.samanthalind.com
samantha@samanthalind.com

Reader Group
Samantha Lind's Alpha Loving Ladies
Good Reads
https://goo.gl/t3R9Vm
Newsletter
https://bit.ly/FDSLNL

facebook.com/SamanthaLindAuthor

x.com/samanthalind1

instagram.com/samanthalindauthor

bookbub.com/authors/samantha-lind

www.ingramcontent.com/pod-product-compliance
Lightning Source LLC
Chambersburg PA
CBHW021708190726
48289CB00008B/2434